U0009675

動物農莊
Animal Farm
中英雙語典藏版

喬治·歐威爾——著

李立瑋——譯　楊宛靜——繪

晨星出版

導讀

文字工作者 伊象菁

　　通往動物農莊的路不是單一的。如果按著前人的定論對號入座，在對照作者歐威爾的企圖之後，或許會有「原來如此」的感受，但那肯定會少了寓言原有的興味。若是按圖索驥地將歷史事件一一明列，只能說是閱讀小說時天馬行空的想像力，恐怕會因而被韁繩勒緊。不過作為通往動物農莊的路徑之一，回過頭來說，動物農莊果真是一個充滿想像力的地方。

　　在談動物農莊一些延伸出來的問題之前，我們先來了解歐威爾當初創作的初衷，亦不失為另一種閱讀的方向，也是許多書評認為動物農莊的最大寓意：針對一九一七年俄國的二月革命到一九四三年底德黑蘭會議的蘇聯歷史，即史達林虛假的社會主義體制以及當時與蘇聯同一陣營的英美等國作出的嚴厲諷刺，希望可以以尖銳的筆觸提醒世人，蘇聯的社會主義不過是披著羊皮的狼，政客們為一己之私，無謂於百姓的苦難，也不察百姓絲毫沒有減少的痛苦。

　　我們也幾乎可以將小說中的人物與事件與現實作一對照。大豬梅傑為列寧，拿破崙為史達林，雪球為托洛斯基。拿破崙手下的九隻惡犬正是俄國國家祕密警察，盲從的羊群為青年共產主義同盟，瓊斯先生被影射為俄國沙皇，狐木農莊的皮爾金頓先生為英國，平徹菲爾德農莊的弗雷德里克先生為德國。小說中最重要的風車為產業五年計畫，還有其它的事件都可以找到對應的現實情況來作一呼應。不過歐威爾雖然是以俄國的社會主義作為諷刺的對象，但事實上最重要的還是要洞悉在整個事件背後所被操控的權力問題。這也是以下所延伸出來的切入點。

　　權力，在此書裡以各種形式呈現。但即使權力改了各種樣貌，由誰來行使，都有著使人著魔與腐化的魔力。不管一開始動物們因為無法忍受權力而鬥爭，或者為了反抗人類剝削而鬥爭，到動物們成功地推翻人類的宰制而得著所謂的自由來說；權力，在鬥爭的過程裡，在鬥爭結束之後，都確實地被所謂的領導者以各種名義行使著，因此在鬥爭之前的私人資本的擁有或者領導者對動物們的控制，在結束鬥爭之後仍舊是存在著。

在這裡我們可以由小說中的情節導出一個食物鏈。權力是抽象的，唯有在被利用時成為具體可陳的事實，而利用者必須藉由私人資本的擁有以及對其他人生活的宰制，以成就他成為領導者，此一唯一獨有的階級。階級的產生必須以暴力形式呈現並維持，透過暴力的行使建立了階級的制度，而知識在本書裡，更是階級的體現，擁有知識者便是領導者，知識象徵權力，因此在本書裡的領導者無不獨攬知識與教育的權力，並以規訓與懲罰替代了原有的溝通與教育。

我們以本書的微言大義來體認這個世界的脈動，將會發現不管是在實行社會主義的國家或者資本主義國家，這個食物鏈緊緊地扣住甚至制約了每個人的生活。但我們必須深刻地思考果真是權力使人腐化嗎？權力是否真如小說之中所陳述，罪惡是本質的存在；或者是擁有權力者使權力腐化了？權力的本質究竟是什麼，或許才是歐威爾最想讓讀者們去思考的問題吧！

以權力的角度閱讀動物農莊或許是很嚴肅的，而且在歐威爾如此明顯的隱喻下，讀者的確也很容易地對號入座。我們或許可以再開啟另一個視窗，再從語言的角度來閱讀這部小說。當我們既定成俗地將豬指涉為貪婪、骯髒的對象時，歐威爾卻將豬打破慣例地另外樹立了一個聰明甚至狡滑的角色時，在閱讀上是否產生了另類的想像空間，這樣的例子在本書中俯拾皆是，很值得用心以自身的經歷去體會小說裡的寓意。

其實最有趣的閱讀方式是根本不要對本書有任何先入為主的想法，就只是去閱讀，看歐威爾如何將每個角色活靈活現地塑造出來。也不要再去想他要諷刺些什麼，歐威爾並沒有要告訴讀者什麼偉大的歷史，而是人性的本質，權力的本質，他們體現在每個人的人生之中，並因之不同。動物農莊其實真的要花點時間，好好地繞繞幾圈的。

第 1 章

　　入夜了，曼諾農莊主人瓊斯先生鎖上了雞舍，卻因為喝得太醉而忘了關上小門。他醉醺醺地穿過院子，提燈的光亮隨之左右搖擺。來到家的後門，甩掉了腳上的靴子，逕自進入洗滌室，從酒桶為自己滿上最後一杯啤酒，一飲而盡。接著，便循著瓊斯夫人的酣聲摸上了床。

　　當臥室的燈光一熄滅，農莊裡便響起了一陣喧鬧。因為流言蜚語已經在白天傳遍整座農莊，獲得「中等白鬃獎」的大豬梅傑，在前一天晚上作了一個怪夢，他急於把夢的內容告知其他動物們。全體動物已經約定，一旦確定瓊斯先生回家休息了，他們就要在大穀倉裡聚會。儘管他參展時的名稱是「威靈頓美神」，動物們都稱他為大豬梅傑，他在農莊的崇高地位，使得每隻動物無不情願犧牲一個小時的睡眠時間來聽聽他到底要說些什麼。

　　在大穀倉一頭築高的平臺上，大豬梅傑安坐在他的草墊上，頭上的橫梁懸著吊燈。大豬梅傑已經十二歲了，近來身

形變了樣，但仍不失爲一頭外型威嚴的豬。儘管他的獠牙從未被截斷，模樣仍慈善和祥。很快地，動物們漸漸聚齊，各按各的習性坐定位。最先到的是三隻狗：藍鈴、傑西和小鉗。然後是一群豬，他們立刻在最靠近平臺的位置上落座。母雞們棲在窗臺，鴿子們則撲撲拍翅飛到橡梁上，綿羊和母牛臥在豬群的後面開始反芻。一同進來的兩匹壯馬是拳師和克羅薇，他們的腳步緩慢，多毛的蹄子小心地踩踏，惟恐傷到躲在牧草下的小動物。克羅薇是一匹已近中年的母馬，自從生了第四匹小駒之後，就再也恢復不了往日的身材。拳師則是一匹高頭大馬，將近有十八個掌寬高，力氣堪抵兩頭普通的馬。他鼻子上的一條白條紋使他看起來有些愚笨可笑，事實上他雖然並不具備一流的智慧，卻眾所公認性格堅韌，工作起來孔武有力。隨後進來的是山羊穆勒和驢子班傑明，班傑明是農莊裡最老的動物，也是脾氣最壞的動物。他很少說話，縱使開了口，也脫不了尖酸刻薄與憤世嫉俗的評論。比如，他會說，上帝給了他一條驅趕蒼蠅的尾巴，但他寧願上帝既沒有創造蒼蠅也沒有創造尾巴。在所有農莊的動物之中，只有他不苟言笑，他說沒有什麼事情值得他發笑。不過值得一提的是，他和拳師非常投合，儘管他從未公開承認，但他們兩個星期天的時候，經常一起在果園後方的小圍場裡消磨時間，肩並肩地吃著草，卻從不說一句話。

兩匹馬才剛找到位置坐下，一群沒了媽媽的小鴨子排成

一列進入了穀倉，輕聲唧唧叫著，尋找合適的落腳處，以防被大動物們踩到。克羅薇伸出前腿當作屏障圈住他們，小鴨子們很快便在裡頭沉沉睡去。白馬莫莉趕在最後一刻忸怩作態地進場，她搖晃著身軀，輕踏著步伐，嘴裡還嚼著一塊糖。她是一匹愚蠢的漂亮母馬，專為瓊斯先生拉座車。她擠到前方賣弄地甩動白色的鬃毛，想吸引大家注意到她那繫在鬃毛辮子上的漂亮紅絲帶。最後進來的是貓，像往常一樣四下張望著找尋最暖和的地方，最後擠在拳師和克羅薇之間。整場演說中她都滿足地發出呼嚕呼嚕的聲音，大豬梅傑說的話，她一個字也沒聽進去。

除了睡在後門梁柱上的烏鴉摩西，所有動物都已到齊。大豬梅傑看大家都已坐定且全神貫注地等待，他清了清嗓子開始講話：「同志們，你們一定都聽說我昨晚的怪夢了。但是，等等再講我的夢，有些事情我想先說。同志們，我的大限將至，但在我死前，我覺得有義務將自己習得的學問傳承下去。我的生命走過了漫漫長路，我在豬圈裡費盡了無窮的思索，我想我已明白生命的真諦，該是時候對你們說了。

「同志們，我們活著究竟是為了什麼？看看吧，我們的生命悲慘、勞苦而短暫。從誕生以來，我們吃飽飯不過是為了能活著呼吸，讓身體能夠繼續幹活，直到用盡最後的一點力氣。當我們不再有用處的時候，就會被殘酷無情地送進屠宰場。在整個英格蘭，只有一歲以下的幼獸才懂得什麼是快

樂，什麼是休閒。在整個英格蘭，沒有一隻動物是自由的。在動物的生命裡只有悲慘和奴役，這就是赤裸裸的現實。

「但這就是命運的安排嗎？這只是因爲我們的土地貧瘠得不能讓棲身於此的子民過上體面的生活？不是的，同志們，絕對不是！我們英格蘭的土地肥沃、氣候宜人，它能供給的食物豐饒，即使住在這的動物再多上幾倍也足夠。單是我們的這個小農莊就足夠養活十二匹馬、二十頭牛和上百隻綿羊──而且，都能過上比現在更舒適、更體面的生活，而且超乎我們的想像。那爲什麼我們仍持續陷在這種悲慘處境呢？因爲人類，我們付出勞動所生產的一切，幾乎全部都被人類偷走了。同志們，這就是問題的答案。歸結成一個詞──人類。人類是我們唯一的敵人。除掉了人類，飢餓和過勞的問題根源也會永遠不再。

「人類是農莊裡唯一只消費不生產的生物。他不產奶，不下蛋，力不能拉犁，跑不能逐兔，但卻是所有動物的主人。他驅使所有動物工作，而他給動物們的食物卻只能勉強不致餓死，自己卻將剩下的都奪走。是我們在辛勤地耕地，是我們的糞便使大地肥沃，而兩手空空的也是我們。奶牛們，去年妳們擠出了成千加侖的奶，而這些本該餵養出強壯牛犢的奶水到哪去了？每一滴都流進了我們敵人的喉嚨裡！母雞們，去年妳們又生了多少個蛋？其中有多少個被孵成了小雞？剩下的都被送到市場上爲瓊斯和他的雇工們換得了錢

幣。還有克羅薇，妳生的四隻小馬都到哪兒去了？有誰來供養和安慰妳的晚年？他們每隻都在剛滿一歲的時候就被賣掉，妳再也不會見到他們。而妳在經歷了四次分娩和在牧場辛勤勞動後又得到了什麼？僅僅是一口糧食和一個窩。

「甚至，我們如此悲慘地生活，還不讓我們安享天年。我是不需為自己抱怨什麼的，畢竟我還算是個幸運的傢伙。我已經十二歲了，有了四百多個子孫。這只是每一頭豬都該享有的正常生活。但是，沒有哪一隻動物最終逃得過刀斧。還有你們，坐在我前方的年輕肉豬們，一年內就會被逼到牆角扯破嗓子叫喊救命。所有動物都會迎來這恐怖的結局，牛、豬、雞、羊。就算是馬跟狗，下場也不會比較好。你，拳師，當你老邁無力的時候，瓊斯先生會毫不猶豫地把你賣給屠馬商，你會被殘忍地割斷喉嚨，你的肉會被熬煮成獵狐犬的食物。狗也無法僥倖逃過，當他們年邁衰老、牙齒掉光時，瓊斯先生會在他們的脖子上繫上磚頭，把他們溺死在最近的湖裡。

「這還不夠清楚嗎？同志們，我們生命中所有的禍害都源自人類的暴政。只有消滅了人類，我們才能真正擁有自己的勞動果實，甚至能在一夜之間變得富有而自由。我們接下來該做什麼？開始不分日夜，身心都投入推翻人類統治的大業！同志們，這就是我要告訴你們的訊息——革命！我不知道革命會在什麼時候開始，也許要等一個星期，也許要等上

一百年，但我清清楚楚地知道，就如同我清楚地看見腳下青草的模樣，正義終將來臨。仔細看吧，也許就在你短暫的餘生裡。並且，把我的意思傳達給你們的後代，讓我們的子子孫孫都為正義而奮鬥，直到正義戰勝的那一刻。

「記住，你們的決心絕不能動搖，任何言論都無法使你偏離正軌。關於那些人類和動物有著共同利益、一榮俱榮的話連聽都不要聽，那全是謊言，人類都是為一己私利著想的。我們動物要團結一致與之戰鬥，所有的人類都是敵人，所有的動物都是戰友。」

這時，聽眾中起了一陣騷動。四隻大老鼠爬出洞來落地而坐聆聽梅傑的演說，狗兒們一眼就看見他們，老鼠只得在一瞬間倉皇逃回洞裡。梅傑舉起豬蹄子要求肅靜。

「同志們，有一點必須要釐清，那些野生動物們，比如老鼠、野兔，究竟是我們的朋友還是敵人？讓我們投票決定吧！我在此提議表決：『老鼠是否為我們的同盟？』」

表決很快地結束了，同意老鼠是朋友的票數獲得壓倒性勝利，只有來自三隻狗和一隻貓的四張反對票，不過大家隨後發現貓在正反方都投了票。

梅傑繼續他的談話：「我要說的已經不多了，只是需要重申，你們要永遠記住，對抗人類和他們的暴行是你們的使

命，兩條腿的是敵人，四條腿或者有翅膀的是朋友。而且，當我們對抗人類時，千萬不能仿效他們的惡行，即便我們征服了他們，也不能承襲他們的惡習。我們不能住在房子裡，不能睡在床上，不能穿衣，不能喝酒，不能抽煙，更不能去沾染銅臭、經商做生意。人類的所有習性都是邪惡的。當然，最重要的是，任何動物都不能稱王稱霸、凌駕於他的同類。無論是弱小的還是強壯的，無論是聰明的還是愚笨的，全都是兄弟。動物絕不能殘殺同類，所有動物都是平等的。

「現在，我該告訴你們昨晚我到底夢見了什麼？這個夢難於描述。它展示了一個未來，一個人類被消滅的未來。它讓我想起我久已忘記的東西。那是很多年以前，當我還是一隻小豬的時候，媽媽和其他母豬們經常唱起的一首老歌——雖然她們只曉得曲調和開頭前三個字。那個曾經熟悉的調子早已被我遺忘，但在昨夜，它重回我的夢裡，甚至歌詞也重回記憶之中。我敢肯定，這首歌很久以前也曾被動物們傳唱，但漸漸消逝於世代的更迭。現在，同志們，我要唱這首歌給你們聽，儘管我年老得嗓音已沙啞，但傳授給你們後，你們會為了自己唱得更好。這首歌叫做**英格蘭之獸**。」

大豬梅傑清了清嗓子就唱了起來。如他所說，他的嗓音確實有些沙啞，但唱得已經夠好了。歌曲的旋律慷慨激昂、激勵人心，類似美國民謠《小姑娘》和墨西哥歌謠《蟑螂》。而它的歌詞是這樣的：

英格蘭之獸，愛爾蘭之獸，
普天之下的野獸們，
請聆聽這喜悅的佳音，
請聆聽那黃金的未來。

那一天遲早會到來，
人類的暴政將被推翻，
英格蘭富饒的大地上，
將只有野獸蹤跡遍布。

鼻子將不再戴有環鈴，
背上也不再配有鞍具，
銜鐵和馬刺會永遠地腐爛，
無情的鞭打聲也不再響起。

超乎想像的富饒生活，
大麥、小麥、燕麥和牧草，
苜蓿、豆糧和甜菜，
那一天都將歸我們所有。

英格蘭的田野將陽光普照，
流水更加清澈，微風更為和煦，
那一天我們將獲得自由。

為了那一天，我們都將奉獻，
哪怕我們等不到自由曙光照耀，
牛，馬，鵝，雞，
都將為自由辛苦奮鬥。

英格蘭之獸，愛爾蘭之獸，
普天之下的野獸們，
請傾聽並傳唱這曲，
傳唱我們的黃金未來。

　　歌曲使所有動物都激動不已，甚至梅傑還沒唱完，他們也跟著曲調哼唱。即使最愚鈍的動物也已學會了曲調、明瞭了大意，聰明者如豬和狗早已在數分鐘內領會整首曲子、熟記在心。終於，初試啼聲之後，農莊裡響徹動物們宏亮的合唱歌聲——牛兒哞哞地叫，狗兒汪汪地吠，羊兒咩咩地鳴，鴨兒呱呱地喚，馬兒希律律地嘶鳴。他們是如此亢奮地齊唱這首歌，還接續唱了五回，若是沒有被打擾中斷，他們恐怕會徹夜唱著。

　　不幸的是，喧鬧聲吵醒了瓊斯先生。他確信是溜進了狐狸，於是匆忙下床，抓起常備在房間角落的槍，向著黑夜連射了六發子彈。子彈卡進了穀倉的牆裡，聚會中的動物們匆忙逃散，大家飛也似地逃回了各自的棲所，鳥兒跳進了窩，動物們安身於稻草堆，農莊一瞬間恢復了往日的寧靜，各自沉沉睡去。

第 2 章

　　三天後，大豬梅傑在睡夢中平靜地死去，遺體被埋在了果園的樹根下。

　　那是三月初的事了，接下來的三個月裡，有許多活動祕密地進行著。農莊裡比較聰明的動物們受梅傑的一番話啓發，有了嶄新的生存觀。雖然他們並不知道梅傑預言的革命會在何時開始，也沒有理由認爲這場革命會在他們有生之年發生，但他們都清楚地知道，爲這場革命鋪路是畢生的責任。宣傳與組織的工作自然地落在了豬的身上，因爲大家公認他們是動物當中最聰慧的。豬群當中，有兩隻公豬最爲出類拔萃，一隻名叫雪球，另一隻名叫拿破崙，都是瓊斯先生準備養大了賣掉的。拿破崙是農莊裡唯一的一隻盤克夏豬，體形碩大，面目有些猙獰，話不多卻眾所皆知固執己見。雪球的性格比較活潑開朗，健談且思想創新，但個性不如拿破崙沉穩。農莊裡的其他公豬都是些食用豬，他們之中最有名的是史奎爾，臉頰圓潤，眼睛炯炯有神，動作敏捷，嗓音尖銳。他是個高明的演說家，當說到一個艱澀難懂的論點時，

他總是來回踱步，不時地揮動著尾巴使其更具說服力。在其他動物的心目中，史奎爾確實有著顛倒黑白的口才。

　　這三隻豬將梅傑的言論發展成了一套完整的思想體系，並為之冠名為「動物主義」。一個星期會有幾晚，在瓊斯先生睡熟的夜裡，他們會在穀倉裡密會，不厭其煩地一遍又一遍地闡述動物主義的精神。起初，他們面臨不少冷淡的態度以及一些惹人發笑的愚蠢問題。有的動物談到了對「主人」瓊斯先生忠誠的義務，或者發表一些幼稚言論：「是瓊斯先生養活我們，如果瓊斯先生不在了，我們一定會餓死。」還有提出諸如此類的問題：「我們為什麼要在乎死後的事情？」或者是：「如果革命注定要發生，那我們做什麼都無關緊要，不是嗎？」因此，三隻豬總是要費盡心力地指出，這些說法都是與動物主義的核心思想背道而馳。最愚蠢的問題都母馬莫莉問的，她問雪球的第一句話是：「革命以後還會有糖吃嗎？」

　　「沒有，」雪球斬釘截鐵地說，「在這片農莊裡，我們沒有製糖的道具。況且，妳並不需要糖，妳會得到所有妳想要的燕麥和牧草。」

　　「那我還能在頭鬃上繫上絲帶嗎？」莫莉又問。

　　「我的同志呀，」雪球說，「妳迷戀的那些絲帶正是奴役的標誌。難道妳不明白，自由的價值是更勝於絲帶的？」

莫莉雖然點點頭，但看上去似乎並沒有認同雪球的話。

更為費力的工作是，三隻豬要忙於撲滅烏鴉摩西到處散播的謊言。摩西是瓊斯先生的寵物，是動物們當中的間諜，專門散播謠言，而且能言善辯。他聲稱有一個神祕的「蜜糖山」，那裡是所有動物死後的歸宿。據摩西說，蜜糖山就坐落在天空，在雲彩後方不遠處。在那裡，一週七日都是星期天，一年四季都生長著繁茂的苜宿，樹籬上長著糖塊和亞麻籽餅。動物們都不喜歡摩西，因為他只會耍嘴皮子，從來不做事。但仍有些動物對蜜糖山抱有堅定的信仰，為此，三隻豬不得不苦口婆心地解釋，說根本不存在這樣的地方。

拳師和克羅薇，這兩匹高壯的拖曳馬是三隻豬最忠實的信徒，他們無法為自己仔細考慮任何事情，但當他們把三隻豬視為師長後，對於三隻豬所說的一切無不照單全收，並用簡單的話把意思傳達給其他動物們。他們從不缺席穀倉裡的祕密會議，散會前總會響起「英格蘭之獸」，都是由他們作為領唱。

關鍵時刻來臨了，誰也沒有料到革命會爆發得如此之早而又如此地輕易。在過去幾年，瓊斯先生雖然算不上是位溫和的主人，但至少還算是個勤勞能幹的農夫，但最近的一段日子裡他過得很糟。他先是在一次訴訟當中損失了一大筆的財產，因而日日借酒澆愁。他會整日倒在廚房的溫莎椅上看

報、喝酒,有時用泡過啤酒的麵包邊餵摩西。農莊裡的雇工們懶散又不老實,田裡荒草叢生,漏雨的屋頂也無人修補,籬笆也缺乏照料,動物們也變得有一頓沒一頓的。

六月來臨,該是收割牧草的時節了。仲夏節前夕,那天是星期六,瓊斯先生醉倒在威靈頓的紅獅酒館,直到第二天的中午才趕回農莊。雇工們一早擠完了奶就外出獵兔子去了,沒人在意動物們還餓著肚子。瓊斯先生一回來就躺到起居室的沙發上,胡亂抓了份《世界新聞報》遮在臉上就一頭睡到晚上,而動物們始終沒有進食。終於,大家實在無法忍受了。先是一頭牛在儲藏屋外,頂著她的牛角破門而入,接著,所有的動物湧入並盡情地從垃圾箱中翻找食物。瓊斯先生這時才醒了過來,急忙和他的四名雇工趕來儲藏屋一起到處胡亂揮舞著鞭子。飢腸轆轆的動物們再也忍無可忍,雖然沒有事先計畫,此刻動物們蜂擁而上,朝他們積怨已久的人類猛撲過去。當瓊斯一夥頓時發現自己身陷蹄子與犄角的包圍,不斷遭到踢打與衝撞,局面已經無法掌控了。動物們從不曾有過這樣的舉動,不管人類如何恣意地毒打與虐待,他們向來逆來順受。如今突如其來的暴動威力竟嚇得瓊斯一夥人魂不附體,不消一兩分鐘的時間,他們便放棄防衛抵抗,拔腿奔逃而去。轉眼間,瓊斯一夥五個人已在通往大路的車道上沒命地飛奔,動物們則以勝利之姿緊追在後。

瓊斯夫人從臥室的窗戶看到了這一切,便匆忙地收拾了

些細軟，放進她的毛氈包裡，從另一條路溜走了。摩西從巢中躍起尾隨在她身後，呱呱大叫著。同一時間，動物們已成功將瓊斯一夥追趕到大路上凱旋歸來，他們關上了農莊的五柵門。

在他們還沒有意會到發生了什麼事前，革命已經成功地結束了。瓊斯一夥被驅逐，曼諾農莊已屬於動物們。

起初，動物們簡直無法相信好運已降臨。第一件事就是全體迅速地搜索整座農莊，以確保沒有人類藏身其中，然後又相繼跑回到農莊房屋裡，清掃消滅所有瓊斯政權的痕跡。馬廄盡頭的工具間被撞開了，馬銜、牛鼻環、狗項圈、還有瓊斯先生用來閹割豬羊的血腥的刀具，通通被扔進了井裡。韁繩、籠頭、眼罩、恥辱的飼料袋，連同皮鞭，也全被扔進了廢料場裡熊熊燃燒的垃圾火堆。當看到皮鞭在火焰中翻騰時，所有的動物都雀躍鼓噪了起來。雪球還把絲帶也扔進了火堆，這些絲帶曾是在趕集的日子裡用來裝飾馬的鬃毛的。

「絲帶，」他說，「也是一種服飾，而服飾正是人類的標誌之一。所有的動物都應是裸身的。」

拳師一聽到這話，連忙把隨身的草帽也扔進了火堆。這草帽是他夏天時為了抵禦蚊蟲入耳而戴的。

在很短的時間之內，動物們毀掉了所有能使他們想起瓊

斯先生的東西。拿破崙又帶領大家來到儲藏屋，給每個動物
發放了雙倍的飼料，每隻狗則獲得兩塊餅乾。然後，他們歡
唱起「英格蘭之獸」，從頭到尾整整唱了七遍，筋疲力盡之
後便倒頭睡去 ── 那酣眠的樣子彷彿此生從未入睡過。

　　但他們還是像往常一樣，清晨時分便醒來了，然後突然
記起了昨日光榮的勝利，便爭相向草場奔去。到草場的路上
有一座可以俯瞰整個農莊的土墩，動物們擠到高處，在清澈
的晨光下四處眺望。是的，眼前所見的一切都是他們的了！
這事實使他們愈想愈開心，興奮得一圈又一圈地跳躍，直要
將自己高高拋到空中般狂喜。他們在露水裡打滾，嘴裡塞滿
了夏天香甜的草葉，他們踩踏黑色土壤濺起土塊，在之間打
滾嗅聞馥郁的香氣。他們再次檢視這整片大地 ── 這耕地、
這草原、這果園、這池塘、這矮林 ── 令他們讚嘆得說不出
話。那神情就好像他們從來沒見過這些美景，甚至直到現在
依然難以置信這一切都已真正地屬於他們了。

　　然後，他們列隊回到了農莊房屋，在農舍的門外停住了
腳步，屏息以待。這農舍也是他們的了，但當真要進去的時
候卻還是有些害怕。然而過了一會兒，雪球和拿破崙終於用
肩膀撞開了大門，動物們魚貫而入，腳步輕怕地生怕驚擾了
什麼。他們踮著腳尖走過一間又一間的房間，除了耳語，不
敢高聲說話，驚嘆地注視著一樣又一樣難以想像的奢侈品：
大床上鋪著用他們的毛絨製成的床墊、精美的鏡子、馬毛填

製的沙發、布魯塞爾地毯、客廳壁爐上維多利亞時代的版
畫……大家正要下樓的時候，發現莫莉不見了。回頭便見莫
莉停留在最好的那間臥室裡，她從瓊斯夫人的梳妝檯上找到
了一條藍色的絲帶，繫在肩上，對著鏡子愚蠢地搔首弄姿。
這樣的舉動招致了大家的一片指責，隨後他們走出屋外。掛
在廚房的一些火腿被拿出來入土埋葬，洗滌室的啤酒桶因為
被拳師踢了一腳而碎了一地，除此之外，農舍裡幾乎沒有被
翻動過。他們當場全體一致通過一個決議：農舍應該保留下
來作為博物館，而且沒有任何動物可以住進那裡。

早餐後，雪球和拿破崙又把大家召集到一起。

「同志們，」雪球說，「現在才剛六點半，離天黑還有
很長一段時間。從現在起，我們要開始收割牧草。但在開始
收割之前，有一件事情要請大家注意。」

豬在這時透露了在過去的三個月裡，他們已經從瓊斯家
小孩扔進垃圾堆的老舊拼字簿裡學會了讀書寫字。拿破崙派
同志弄來幾罐黑色和白色的油漆桶，帶領大家走到那扇通往
外邊大路的五柵大門前。因為雪球的書寫能力最好，他抓起
一把刷子，將刷子夾在他蹄子趾頭間，把大門上第一根木條
上「曼諾農莊」幾個字抹掉，隨後寫上了四個大字——動物
農莊。農莊今後就叫這個名字了。這之後他們回到農莊建
築，雪球跟拿破崙又派同志弄來一把梯子架在大穀倉牆上，

他們解釋通過三個月來的學習，他們把動物主義歸納成了
「動物七誡」，這七誡將被刻在牆上，在動物農莊裡生活的
動物此後都要遵守這七誡，形成堅定不移的戒律。雪球費力
地爬上梯子，對於一頭豬而言，在梯子上保持平衡可真不是
件容易的事。雪球開始落筆，史奎爾在幾階下為他舉著油漆
桶。在油黑的牆面上，「七誡」是用巨大的白字寫成的，在
三十碼外都能辨識。它的內容是這樣的：

動物七誡

1. 凡是有兩條腿的都是敵人
2. 凡是有四條腿的或是有翅膀的都是朋友
3. 動物不准穿衣
4. 動物不准睡床
5. 動物不准喝酒
6. 動物不准殺害同類
7. 所有動物一律平等

雪球的字跡整齊美觀，除了「朋友」寫成了「友朋」，還有「人」上下顛倒外，其他的字都寫得相當正確。雪球對著全體動物又高聲朗讀了一遍，動物們紛紛點頭稱是，聰明一點的已經立刻用心背誦了。

「現在，同志們，」雪球扔掉了手裡的刷子後高聲喊道，「到草原去吧！事關我們動物的榮耀，讓我們收割得比瓊斯他們更快！」

但在此時，那三頭奶牛卻不安分起來，他們似乎已經焦慮了好一陣子，開始大聲地哞哞叫著。因為她們已經整整二十四個小時沒有擠奶，她們的乳房簡直要漲破了。只花了幾秒的思考時間，三隻豬便叫同志拿來了大桶子，並相當順利地為奶牛擠奶，也因此才發現豬蹄子竟然很適合這項工作。很快地就有了五大桶還浮著泡沫、濃郁香甜的鮮奶，所有動物都不由得眼巴巴地望著。

某個聲音忍不住了：「我們怎麼處置這些牛奶呢？」

「瓊斯先生有時會摻一些牛奶在我們的飼料裡。」一隻母雞說。

「不要在意這些牛奶，同志們，」拿破崙一邊說一邊用身體擋住了大桶子，「那個之後會處理，現在，收割才是更重要的。雪球同志會在前面指引大家，我幾分鐘後就到。前

進吧,同志們!牧草在等著我們!」

　　於是,動物們行軍般衝到草原裡開始收割。當他們黃昏歸來的時候,牛奶卻神祕地消失了。

第 3 章

　　為了收割牧草並拖回農莊,他們有多麼的勤奮努力,揮灑了多少的汗水。但這些努力都沒有白費——牧草的收穫遠遠超出了預期的量。

　　有時候工作起來很辛苦費力,因為收割器材是專為人類所設計,並不適合動物們,而且他們無法用後腿站立,這一點相當不利於使用器具。但三隻豬充分發揮了他們的聰明才智,克服了一切的困難。對於馬來說,他們熟悉這裡每一英寸的土地,事實上在割草和耙地這方面還比瓊斯那些人更在行。三隻豬並不真正參與勞動,只是負責指導和監督。由於他們有著優越的知識,他們理所當然地獲得了領袖的地位。拳師和克羅薇會自行操作著收割機和馬拉耙,當然,此時已經不再需要銜鐵和韁繩了。當他們在耕地裡步伐穩健地大步繞行一圈又一圈時,會有隻豬在身後吆喝:「前進,同志!」有時候會是「後退,同志!」所有動物都不遺餘力地運送牧草,甚至鴨子和母雞也整日一次次地銜著草葉往返奔波。最後,他們只花了整整兩天的時間就完成收割,比過去

瓊斯一夥人還要來得有效率多了。而且，這還是農莊有史以來最豐收的一次。也沒有絲毫的浪費，就連最小的草梗也逃不過鴨子和母雞們銳利的眼睛，甚至沒有任何動物妄想過偷吃一口。

　　整個夏天，農莊裡的工作就像鐘錶一樣按部就班。動物們從未想過能夠過得如此地快樂，每嚼一口食物都是無比地享受。因為吃的是真正屬於自己的食物，為了自己耕耘收穫的食物，而不再是來自一位吝嗇主人的施捨。人類才是農莊的寄生者，現在毫無用處的人類已經不在了，每隻動物都可以分到更多的食物。閒暇的時光也多了起來，雖然動物們還不太適應。他們也遇到了無數的困難，比如，年底收割穀物的時候，因為農莊裡並沒有脫粒機，他們必須用很原始的方法一點點地吹掉稻殼。但幸好，三隻豬的智慧和拳師驚人的蠻力足以克服一切的困難。拳師是大家崇敬的對象，他在瓊斯時代就已經贏得了勤勞的名聲，如今他工作起來彷若有三匹馬的力量。會有些時日，整個農莊的重擔似乎都壓在了他寬大的肩膀上。從早到晚他從不停歇，而且總是出現在工作最繁重的地方。他特別請一隻小公雞在其他動物起床前半小時就叫醒他，甚至在日常工作開始之前，志願做最需要苦力的工作。他遇到困難或挫折時，總是告訴自己：「我會更加努力工作。」——這已經成了他的座右銘。

　　每一隻動物都盡其所能地工作，例如母雞和鴨子們，連

同撿拾零星的穀粒，便收獲了百來公升的食糧。在這裡，沒有誰偷竊，沒有誰抱怨沒得到足夠的食物配給；在瓊斯時代屢見不鮮的爭吵、撕咬、嫉妒幾乎都已經絕跡。也沒有誰偷懶逃避工作——「幾乎」沒有。莫莉總是起得晚、離開得早——以石頭卡在她的馬蹄裡為由；貓的行為也有些離奇，在工作場合經常找不到她，她會一連消失幾個小時，到了吃飯的時間或是一天的工作已經完成時才若無其事地突然露面。她總是能找出無數個精彩絕倫的藉口，發出得人疼的呼嚕聲，讓人無法不相信她的缺席完全是出於好意。老驢班傑明在革命之後似乎沒有絲毫的改變，他依然頑固地保持著在瓊斯時代就已養成的慢吞吞作風，既不偷懶少做，也不自願多做。對於革命和革命的結果，班傑明沒有發表任何高見。當問及他是否對瓊斯先生被驅逐一事感到高興，他總是給出一個讓人摸不著頭腦的答案：「驢的壽命太長了，你們沒有人看過死驢。」其他的動物也不得不停止追問，接受這神祕的回答。

星期天是休息的時間，早飯比平常要晚一個小時，飯後有個每星期都會舉行的例行儀式。先是升旗，雪球在工具間裡找到了瓊斯夫人的一塊綠色桌巾，在上面用白色顏料畫上了一隻蹄子和一隻角。每個星期天早晨，這面旗幟都會在農莊的花園中高高升起。旗幟是綠色的，雪球解釋這代表了英格蘭的綠色田野，蹄子和角標誌著未來崛起的動物共和：到

了那時，動物們將會是這片大地上真正的主人，而人類的政
權已被澈底推翻。升旗之後，所有的動物列隊走進穀倉舉行
眾所周知的全體集會，制定下週的工作計畫和提案、討論。
提出決議提案的總是那幾隻豬，其他的動物僅僅懂得投票表
決，從來不懂得提出自己的決議。雪球和拿破崙是最熱中於
討論的活躍份子，但他們兩個的意見卻從來沒有一致過。不
管其中一方提出的建議是甚麼，總是遭到另一方毫不留情的
反對。甚至是那種已經通過的，像是把果園後的一小塊圍場
設為已老得不能工作的動物們的休息間，這實際上誰都不反
對，他們也能為每種動物的退休年紀而激烈爭辯。會議照例

都是以合唱「英格蘭之獸」作結，散會後的下午就是娛樂的時間了。

　　豬把工具間當作了他們自己的高層會議室。晚上，他們會在這裡學習書中關於冶鐵、木工和其他技術的各種知識，書是他們從農舍裡拿出來的。雪球除了授課閱讀與書寫外，還忙於組織其他動物成立「動物委員會」，並為此孜孜不倦。他給母雞們成立了「下蛋委員會」，給母牛成立了「淨尾聯盟」，給綿羊們成立了「白羊毛運動」，還成立了「田野同志再教育委員會」，這個委員會的目的是馴服老鼠和野兔，還有其他各式各樣的組織。總體來說，這些專案全部以失敗告終。以馴服野外動物的目標來說，幾乎立刻就失敗了，他們的行為一如既往，對他們慷慨就等著被占便宜，貓參加了「田野同志再教育委員會」，而且在前一些日子裡非常活躍。有天大家看到她坐在屋頂上和麻雀說話，麻雀站在她搆不著的地方。她說現在所有的動物都已是同志了，所以，她非常歡迎任何麻雀到她的腳爪上休息。但儘管如此，麻雀還是警戒地與她保持距離。

　　不過讀寫班卻獲得了巨大的回響。到了秋天，幾乎每一隻農莊裡的動物都能夠在一定程度上識文斷字。

　　至於豬，他們的讀寫能力已經到了相當高的水準。狗的閱讀能力也已經稱得上高超，但除了「七誡」，他們對任何

文字都提不起興趣。山羊穆勒閱讀能力比狗更好,有時候會在晚上,把從垃圾堆撿來的零星報紙唸給其他動物聽。班傑明的閱讀能力一點也不比豬遜色,但卻從不活用展現他的本事。他說據他所知,實在是沒有什麼東西值得一讀。克羅薇認識了全部的字母,卻始終拼不出一個完整的單詞。拳師會用他的大蹄子在土壤上畫出「ㄅ、ㄆ、ㄇ、ㄈ」,但總是停留在注音「ㄈ」,他耳朵豎起,目不轉睛地盯著注音,甚至甩動他額頭上的鬃毛,儘管他費盡心思要想起接下來的注音符號,但都沒有成功。有幾次他居然記住了「ㄉ、ㄊ、ㄋ、ㄌ」,但馬上發現又把「ㄅ、ㄆ、ㄇ、ㄈ」給忘掉了。最後他決定對這四個注音感到心滿意足,每天還要默寫兩次來鞏固記憶。而莫莉呢,除了拼寫自己名字的注音之外,什麼都不願去學。她會用樹枝整齊地排列她的名字,再用一兩朵花裝飾,然後圍著這些樹枝轉圈讚賞一番。

農莊裡的其他動物都只是記下了注音「ㄅ」。此外,一些比較笨的動物——比如綿羊、母雞和鴨子根本連「七誡」都背不起來。有鑒於此,雪球把「七誡」進一步歸納成一句格言:「四條腿的是好漢,兩條腿的是壞蛋」。他說,這一句話涵蓋了動物主義的精髓。

只要能夠真正領悟這句話的真理,就能遠離人類的邪惡影響。鳥第一個就跳出來抗議,因為他們也只有兩條腿。但雪球隨後證明他們不是兩條腿的壞蛋。

「同志們，鳥的翅膀，」他說，「翅膀是幫助身體前進的器官，而不是拿來操控他人，功用和腿是一樣的。人類和我們最大的區別是手，憑著手，他們幹盡了一切壞事。」

鳥兒並不明白雪球的長篇大論，但終究接受了他的解釋。所有較愚鈍的動物都開始口讀心誦這句新的格言：「四條腿的是好漢，兩條腿的是壞蛋」這句話被刻在穀倉的牆上，在「七誡」的上方，字體也更大。一旦綿羊記住了這句話後，便愈發展現對這句話的獨特喜好，一有機會在院子裡躺著休息時便開始咩咩叫著這句話，喋喋不休，從不厭倦。

拿破崙對雪球的委員會毫無興趣，他說年輕人的教育是遠比對成年人的教育還重要。收割結束後沒多久，傑西和藍鈴共產下了九隻健康強壯的小狗。小狗們才剛斷奶，拿破崙就把他們從媽媽的身邊帶走，說是要親自負責對他們的教育。他把他們帶到工具間的閣樓上，必須架上梯子才能上

去。教育的過程是如此地隱祕，以致動物們很快就忘記了這些小狗的存在。

而之前消失的牛奶下落也終於水落石出，原來牛奶每天都被混雜在豬食當中了。

是蘋果成熟的季節了，被風吹落的果實落滿了果園的土地。動物們理所當然地認為這些會平均分配給大家，然後有一天卻來了一道命令，要把這些蘋果收集起來通通送到工具間，專門讓豬享用。對此，有一些動物議論紛紛，但這不影響所有豬都一致贊同的決議，甚至雪球與拿破崙也不例外。最後，史奎爾被委派出去向大家做些必要的解釋。

「同志們！」他喊道，「我希望你們不要以為我們這樣做是出於自私和特權。事實上，我們大多並不喜歡牛奶和蘋果，像我就不喜歡。我們這樣做無非是為了維持身體健康，

而牛奶和蘋果含有一些對豬很有益處的物質，同志們，這是經科學證實的。我們豬是腦力工作者，整個農莊的組織與管理工作都要仰賴我們，我們日夜傾心為大家謀福利。我們喝牛奶、吃蘋果實際都是為了你們好，難道你們不知道如果我們失職意味著什麼？瓊斯會回來的！是的，瓊斯會回來的！是的，同志們！」史奎爾幾近懇求地喊道，同時踱著步晃著尾巴，「你們當中肯定沒有人願意看到瓊斯回來吧？！」

如果有一件事大家一致認同與肯定的，那就是他們絕不希望瓊斯回來。現在既然史奎爾話都說到這份上了，大家也無話可說，因為，顯然確保豬的健康實在是至關重要的事。所以在沒有進一步的討論之下，大家就如此達成共識了，牛奶和蘋果，無論是成熟收成的蘋果還是被風吹落的蘋果，今後都是豬的禁臠。

第 4 章

到了夏末，關於動物農莊的各種消息已經傳遍了整個英格蘭大地。每天，雪球和拿破崙都要把信鴿放飛出去，指示他們與鄰近農莊的動物來往，傳播革命的消息和教唱「英格蘭之獸」。

在這段時間裡，瓊斯先生總是泡在威靈頓的紅獅酒吧裡啜飲。被一群他覺得沒用處的動物趕出自己的農場，遭逢此不公義的殘暴行為，使他受盡折磨。只要有人願意傾聽，他便會訴苦一番。其他農場主人，出於原則都會給予同情，但卻沒有人提供幫助。他哪裡知道，別的農莊主們暗忖的只是如何從中趁火打劫，撈上一把。但不幸中的大幸是，臨近動物農莊的另外兩座農莊一直都不太景氣。其中之一是狐木農莊，面積大，有些荒廢，風格老舊，雜草叢生。牧場不堪使用，籬笆年久失修。農莊主的名字叫皮爾金頓，性格非常隨和，每當季節一到，總是寧願把大部分時間花在釣魚和打獵這些樂趣上。另外一座農莊叫做平徹菲爾德，面積較小，但情況稍微好一點，屬於弗雷德里克先生。他總是面孔嚴峻、

算計精明，彷彿一年到頭都是官司纏身，以討價還價的手段
聞名。這兩位農莊主素來不睦，即使有共同利益可尋也無法
達成一致的意見。

　　儘管如此，這回他們都被動物農莊的革命行動給嚇住
了，惟恐自己農莊裡的動物也會隨之效仿。一開始，他們假
裝對動物自己經營農莊這件事嗤之以鼻。他們本以為這場鬧
劇不出兩週就會結束，還仍固執地稱農場為「曼諾農莊」，
他們沒辦法忍受「動物農莊」這名字。甚至到處造謠說曼諾
農莊裡的動物們陷入無止盡的爭鬥，很快地便飢餓至死。隨
著時間過去，事實證明動物們並沒有餓死自己，弗雷德里克
和皮爾金頓話鋒一轉又稱，如今動物農莊邪惡猖狂，奉行同
類相食，會拿燒得通紅的馬蹄鐵相殘折磨，甚至共享一妻。
他們說，這就是違反自然法則，造反革命的下場！

　　然而，那些謠言從未被當真。關於那座理想農莊的傳
言，說著動物把人類給攆走，自己掌管打理農莊事務，隨著
口耳相傳，持續以不同版本的消息傳遞，有的模糊不清，有
的還走了樣。那一年，革命的風潮席捲了整個大地。一向馴
順的公牛突然變得兇殘，綿羊衝破藩籬就為了狼吞虎嚥苜
蓿，母牛也紛紛踢翻盛裝牛奶的水桶，獵獸們抗拒圍補、把
背上的騎師甩一邊去。「英格蘭之獸」的旋律與字句以驚人
的傳播速度響徹了每一個角落。人類雖然指斥這首歌曲的荒
謬，但在聽到它時又每每壓抑不住心頭的怒火。他們不明

白，動物們怎麼能唱出這樣卑劣的垃圾曲調？所以，一發現有哪隻動物在唱歌，人類馬上就加以鞭撻。但狂熱歌聲勢不可擋，黑鳥兒在籬笆上啾啾唱著，鴿子在樹梢上咕咕哼著。旋律溜進了教堂的鐘響聲裡，溜進了鐵匠鋪的喧囂聲裡。像是預言人類未來的喪鐘，使得人類一聽到便會悄然顫抖。今日喪鐘長鳴，明朝厄運當頭。

十月初，穀子已收割完了，有些已經脫粒完成，儲藏的工作正在進行當中。一個早晨，鴿子疾飛竄天，然後亢奮地降落在動物農莊的院子裡——瓊斯一夥和六名來自狐木農莊和平徹菲爾德農莊的幫手，已經進入五柵門，正沿著車道走向動物農莊。他們全副武裝，手拿棍棒，除了瓊斯，他手中握有一把槍，看樣子是決心要奪回農莊了。

這是早在意料之中的事，動物們不懈怠地準備好應戰。雪球之前在農舍找到了一本描述裘里斯·凱薩軍事行動的舊書中，他從中學會了種種攻殺戰守的方法，於是他負起組織籌備防禦工作的責任。在他迅速地調兵遣將之下，大家很快便就戰鬥位置。

在瓊斯他們一接近農莊房屋的那一刻，雪球便發動了第一輪攻擊——所有的鴿子，一共有三十五隻，全都飛上半空中來回盤旋，然後在瓊斯他們的頭上拉起屎來。正當人類忙著應付鴿子們的空襲時，藏匿在籬笆後面的鵝群衝了出來，

猛烈地啄擊他們的小腿肚。

　　然而這只是一場小規模的狙擊，目的是爲了製造一點騷亂，鵝群很快就被瓊斯他們用木棍驅散了。就在這時，雪球發動了第二波進攻。穆勒、班傑明和整個羊群在雪球的帶領下發動攻勢，從四面八方戳刺撞擊，班傑明轉身抬起他小小的後腳，對瓊斯他們一陣猛踢。可是，這幫揮舞著棍棒、踢著釘鞋的人類，哪是動物們能擊退的。突然，隨著雪球厲聲長叫，動物們得到信號便轉身撤退，從大門退進了院子裡。

　　瓊斯一行人爲勝利大聲歡呼。他們看到動物們如預期般落荒而逃，於是鼓噪一番，胡亂地朝抱頭鼠竄的動物追去。沒想到，這正落入了雪球精心設計的圈套。瓊斯一夥剛剛追進院子裡，在牛棚埋伏已久的三匹馬、三頭母牛和其他的豬立即從他們身後包抄過來，截斷後路。此時，雪球以迅雷不急掩耳的速度發出攻擊指令，雪球自己率先直撲瓊斯本人。瓊斯見狀開槍，子彈劃過了雪球的脊背，噴濺出一道血後，一隻綿羊應聲倒地。雪球毫不遲疑，碩大的身體猛的撞向瓊斯的腿。瓊斯被這股蠻力推進了糞堆，槍也甩了出去。

　　但最怵目驚心的場面當屬拳師了。拳師揚起他的後腿，那被釘上馬刺的巨大蹄腳重重一踢，力道強大到猶如一隻勇猛威武的種馬。他踢碎了狐木農莊的年輕馬夫的腦袋，小夥子的屍體就落在了泥巴裡。親眼目睹的人們嚇得發慌了，紛

紛丟掉手中的武器，下一刻便見他們被所有動物追逐得在院子裡倉皇奔逃。動物們或踢、或咬、或踩、或撞，各自用自己的方式來發洩復仇的快感。就連貓也從屋頂跳下來加入攻擊，她跳到一個牧牛人的肩膀上，在他驚恐的尖叫聲中抓破了他的脖子。終於，這些人總算是奪路逃了出來，沒命地奔逃。人類的掠奪之戰不過維持了五分鐘，便顏面盡失地原路撤退，鵝群追在身後沿路嘶嘶怒叫，猛啄攻擊他們的小腿。

所有的人都逃光了，除了泥巴中臉部朝地的一具屍體。拳師在院子裡試圖用蹄子將他翻身，但屍體沒有任何反應。

「他死了，」拳師有些悲傷，「我不是故意的，我忘了我的蹄上有馬刺。有誰會相信我真的不是故意的？」

「同志，別感情用事！」雪球喊道，他的背上還淌著血，「戰爭就是戰爭，只有死人才不會給我們帶來傷害。」

「我不想殺生，即便是人類，我也不想取走他的性命！」拳師重複道，眼裡噙滿淚水。

「莫莉在哪兒？」有個聲音突然喊道。

莫莉失蹤了。大家一陣驚慌，怕她也許被人類打傷了，或是被人抓走了。最後，大家在馬廄裡找到了莫莉——她把頭深深地埋在飼料槽的乾草堆裡。是的，從槍聲一響她就這樣躲了起來。大家鬆了口氣，回到院子時，卻發現那個「死

人」其實只是昏了過去，剛剛已經甦醒並且逃掉了。

此時動物們欣喜若狂地齊聚一堂，每一位都扯著嗓子吹噓著自己的赫赫戰功，隨即舉辦為勝利喝采的慶祝活動。高高揚起旗幟，一遍又一遍地縱情歌唱著「英格蘭之獸」，大家還為死於槍彈的那隻綿羊舉行了莊嚴的葬禮，並把一棵山楂樹種在他的墓地上。隨後，雪球在墳墓旁簡短地講了些話，強調如有必要，所有動物都應不惜犧牲生命來保衛這座得來不易的動物農莊。

大家一致決定製作榮譽勳章來獎賞有功將士，他們授予雪球和拳師「動物英雄好漢一級勳章」。勳章是銅製的——就是些在工具間裡找到的一些老舊的黃銅馬飾。他們要在星期日或節日時配戴，同時追封二級勳章給那隻死去的綿羊。

為這場戰役命名的討論上起了一些爭執。最終決議命名為「牛棚之役」，因為至關重要的那場伏擊就是在牛棚發起的。之後他們在泥塘裡找到了瓊斯先生的槍，而補給彈匣就在農舍裡。動物們將槍放在了旗杆下方，決定將槍作為禮炮，一年當中要鳴槍兩次：一次是在十月十二日，「牛棚之役」的紀念日；另一次是在仲夏節，革命紀念日。

第 5 章

　　冬天近了，莫莉變得愈來愈惹人嫌。她總要在每天早晨
幹活的時候遲到，還總是振振有辭地說是不小心睡過了頭。
她一天到晚地抱怨這兒疼那兒疼，食欲卻依然旺盛。她會找
出種種藉口溜到飲水池邊，愚痴地低頭盯著倒影顧影自憐。
但比起這些，有些傳聞聽起來更為嚴重了。

　　一天，莫莉在院子裡面心情愉悅地閒逛，擺弄著她的長
尾巴，嘴裡還嚼著一稈乾草，克羅薇突然將她拉至一旁。

　　「莫莉，」她說，「我有件重要的事要告訴妳。今天早
上，在動物農莊和狐木農莊的交界，我看見妳在圍籬那，皮
爾金頓先生的夥計在另外一邊。儘管我離得遠，但我很肯定
我看見他在跟妳說話，然後妳還讓他摸妳的鼻子。告訴我，
莫莉，這到底是怎麼回事？」

　　「什麼怎麼回事？他沒摸，我更沒讓他摸，根本是妳胡
編亂造！」莫莉氣憤得抬起前腿，高高地騰起，接著重重踏
回地面。

「莫莉，看著我，妳敢向我發誓那人沒摸過你的鼻子？」

「當然沒有！」莫莉重複說道，但眼神閃躲著克羅薇，她無法直視克羅薇。下一刻她便飛也似的奔向田野，轉眼就沒了蹤影。

望著莫莉的離去，克羅薇的心頭忽然閃過一個念頭。她沒有對誰提起，徑直跑到莫莉的廄棚裡，用蹄子在草間翻找——草下竟藏著一堆方糖和幾條五彩繽紛的絲帶。

三天後，莫莉不見了，接連幾個星期下落不明。後來還是鴿子傳來了消息，說是在威靈頓那兒見過她。那時，她正給一輛馬車駕轅。那是一輛很時髦的車，漆得光鮮亮麗，正停在一間酒吧門口。一個紅臉的胖子穿著方格子馬褲和高筒靴，看起來像是酒吧的老闆，一邊撫摸莫莉的鼻子一邊餵糖給她。她的棕毛修剪一新，額頭還佩著一條鮮紅的絲帶，據鴿子的說法，她一副志得意滿的樣子。從此以後，再沒有哪隻動物會提起莫莉了。

一月份的天氣惡劣異常，田地硬得像一塊鐵板，任何開墾工作都變得徒勞無功。穀倉裡召開了無數次的會議，聰明的豬都在忙於籌劃下一個季度的工作。他們的聰明使他們成為整個農莊裡當之無愧的最高決策者，儘管他們的決策還需要經過全體動物的投票表決才能獲得通過。要是雪球和拿破

崙之間沒有那麼多摩擦，這樣的決策方式會進行得相當流暢。但每項決議都有論點能引發對方的反駁。當一方建議應該擴大燕麥的種植面積，另一方肯定會說多種大麥才是真正的當務之急；當一方如果說某某地方最適合高麗菜的生長，另一方就非要說除了番薯以外那裡什麼也長不了。他們兩個各自有自己的擁護者，有時兩派意見會爭辯得相當激烈。雪球口才極佳，滔滔的雄辯極具說服力，通常能獲得多數動物的支持；而拿破崙更擅長於休息時間遊說拉取選票。拿破崙的手腕在羊群那裡獲得了巨大成功，後來，不管場合是否合適，羊群都會咩咩地叫著：「四條腿是好漢，兩條腿是壞蛋。」並經常藉機在會議上喊出口號擾亂秩序，特別是在雪球演說到至關重要的部分時，便出聲打斷。雪球曾在農舍裡找到一些過期的《農夫和畜牧業者》雜誌，並對此進行了深入的研究，因而腦中滿是改善與革新技術的想法。當他談起農田排水、飼料保鮮、鹼性爐渣之類的話題時總是頭頭是道，一副知識淵博的樣子。他還規劃了一套複雜的制度，要動物們每天在農地裡不同的地方直接排泄，這樣可以大大省去繁重的運送工作。

拿破崙在這一方面毫無建樹，總在背後偷偷說雪球的這些伎倆最後都免不了是竹籃打水一場空。看來，拿破崙是在騎驢看唱本，等待時機。然而，在他們無休無止的爭論當中，最為激烈的應當是關於風車的那次了。

在離農場建築不遠處，有塊占地狹長的牧場，那有一座小山丘，是整個農莊最高的地方。在詳盡的勘察之後，雪球向大家宣布說沒有什麼地方能比那裡更適合建造風車了。這個風車可以帶動發電機，可以為農莊提供電力，這樣馬廄牛棚裡就能用上電燈照明，冬天還能取暖，也可以使用電鋸、鍘草機、甜菜切片機和電動擠奶機等，都是些動物們前所未聞的東西。因為這座農莊比較老舊，只有一些老掉牙的機器。動物們目瞪口呆地聽著雪球繪聲繪影地描述這些機器，這些機器能讓他們悠閒地吃著草，還能讓他們多出時間讀書談天，精進學習。

不出幾個星期，雪球的風車設計方案就全部擬訂完成。技術方面的詳細資料大多取自於瓊斯先生的三本書：《一千個蓋房子的有用技巧》、《人人都是砌磚工》和《電力學入門》。

雪球把孵蛋用的棚子當作自己的工作間，棚子內光滑的木質地板，可以用來繪製設計圖。他時常在裡頭閉門造車，一待就是好幾個小時。他會將書攤開，用石塊壓著，兩趾之間夾著一截粉筆，他在裡頭來回快速移動腳步，一筆一筆地勾勒出雛形，他邊畫邊自顧自地讚嘆出聲。漸漸地，設計圖出現大量的曲軸和齒輪，圖面複雜到需要大半個地板空間。這對其他動物們來說簡直太深奧了，但仍為此感到欽佩，每天至少都要來看一次雪球畫圖。就連平時不問世事的雞和鴨

子也來了，並且還小心翼翼地不去踩踏到地上的那些粉筆
線。

　　只有拿破崙自始至終都漠不關心，他打從一開始就聲明
對風車計畫持反對意見。儘管如此，他還是在某一天突如其
來地造訪雪球的工作間，檢視風車設計圖。他在棚子裡重重
地來回踱步踩踏，仔細查看每一處細節，偶爾會冷哼兩聲，
然後站在一旁斜眼凝視。突然，他抬起腿來，對著設計圖撒
了一泡尿，然後一聲不吭，揚長而去。

　　動物們在風車一事上截然分成了兩派。雪球毫不掩飾，
坦承建造風車的工程繁重，需要運石築牆，還要製作運轉葉
片，之後甚至需要發電機和電纜──這些東西該怎麼製造，
雪球倒是沒有說明。但他堅持認為，整個工程可以在一年之
內完成，而且信誓旦旦地聲稱，風車的建造完成後，將能節
省大量的勞力，動物們每個星期就只需要工作三天了。拿破
崙的觀點卻截然不同，他以為當前最緊要的是迅速增加糧食
生產，如果不明智地在風車上浪費時間，那到時候大家就只
有餓死一途。就這樣，動物間出現了兩派不同的口號，分別
是「擁護雪球的每週三天工作制」和「擁護拿破崙的糧食滿
倉制」。班傑明是唯一不選邊站的動物，對誰的話都不信，
無論是糧食會豐足不缺，或是風車能節省大量勞動力。他
說，不管有沒有風車，生活都會一如往常地繼續，繼續糟糕
地過下去。

除了風車問題的歧見爭執外，農莊的防禦力問題也困擾大家已久——儘管瓊斯一夥在「牛棚之役」中大敗而歸，但動物們都清楚知道，這不會輕易消弭人類嘗試奪回農莊的決心，甚至會更加堅決地幫助瓊斯先生復辟掌權。畢竟「牛棚之役」的消息已經傳遍了全國，使得鄰近農莊裡的動物們變得比以往難以駕馭，人類也因此更有理由要扳回一城。不過雪球和拿破崙一如往常地為此事爭論。根據拿破崙的意見，動物們的當務之急就是迅速把自己武裝起來，並且學習怎樣使用武器；而雪球卻說，他們更應該放出更多的鴿子，到其他的農莊裡去煽動革命。拿破崙主張如果不增強防衛能力，就等於坐以待斃；雪球則認為如果點燃革命之火，使其蔓延至全國各地，硝煙四起，他們也就沒有自我防衛的必要了。動物們一開始贊同拿破崙的說法，後來也覺得雪球的話不無道理。的確，他們總是輕易地搖擺自己的觀點，取決於當下是誰在發表高見。

雪球的設計圖終於完成了，但是否真的要開工建造則還要等到在星期天的大會上表決。那一天，面對聚集到穀倉裡的全體動物，雪球起身闡明他之所以提倡風車建造計畫的緣由——雖然期間他被綿羊的咩咩聲打斷了幾次。接著，拿破崙站起來反駁，他語氣平和地說風車計畫很荒唐，要大家不要把票投給雪球，話才講不到三十秒便迅速坐下，看似不在乎眼前毫無反應的群眾。此時雪球為了爭取大家的認同，猛

地站起身來，隨即大聲喝止又開始咩咩亂叫的羊群，再度慷慨激昂地呼籲。在這之前，動物們因為各有所好，兩邊的支持數量相當，但此刻全被雪球極富感染力的論述所折服。雪球熱切地描述未來的嶄新氣象，動物們的重擔將不復在，農莊生活將會多麼愜意。他構想的畫面早已不再只有鋤草機和切蘿蔔機。他說，有了電能就能使用脫粒機、耕耘機、碎土機、碾米機、收割機和捆紮機。除此之外，還能讓每一個窩棚裡都能用上電燈和冷熱水，甚至是電暖爐。當他描繪完未來的藍圖時，全體動物們的心之所向已一目了然。但就在這個關頭，拿破崙忽然站了起來，不懷好意地瞥了雪球一眼，發出一聲尖銳的嚎叫，沒有動物聽過他發出那樣的聲音過。

此時外面傳來一陣兇狠的吠叫聲，緊接著，九條大狗，戴著鑲有銅釘的項圈，衝進大穀倉裡，徑直撲向雪球。就在這千鈞一髮之際，雪球跳起來躲過他們的利齒，沒幾秒便逃出門外，九條狗在後頭窮追不捨。動物們都被這景象嚇呆了，一個個張口結舌，紛紛湧出門外觀看這場追逐。雪球使出渾身解數飛奔著，穿過通往大路的狹長牧場，而九條狗就快要逮到他時，突然間他滑倒了，眼看小命就要不保了。可他又趕緊爬了起來，飛奔得比以往更快了，正當狗又要再次追上時，其中一條狗幾乎就要咬住雪球的尾巴了，幸而雪球及時把尾巴甩開。接著又是一陣衝刺狂奔，和狗不過一步之差時，從樹籬中的一個洞口竄了出去，再也不見蹤影。

　　餘悸猶存的動物們這才不發一語地回到穀倉。不一會兒，那些狗又汪汪地叫著跑了回來。一開始，誰都想不透這些凶巴巴的傢伙是從哪兒鑽出來的，但謎底很快就揭曉了——他們正是早先被拿破崙從他們母親身邊帶走的那些幼犬，一直被拿破崙偷偷地豢養著。儘管還沒有完全長大，但個頭都已經不算小了，看上去簡直凶狠得像狼。大家也都注意到，他們始終緊挨著拿破崙，對他親暱地擺著尾巴。那模樣竟和過去別的狗對瓊斯先生展現的熱情一模一樣。

　　這時，拿破崙在那些忠狗的簇擁下，登上了大豬梅傑當年發表演說的平臺，高聲宣布，星期天的大會毫無必要，只是浪費時間而已，所以將從此取消。往後所有農莊的議題，將由豬組成的特別委員會集體定奪，他會親自掌管主持。委員會私下開會達成的決議，都會在後會通知其他動物。但動物們仍要在星期天早晨集合，舉行升旗儀式，歌唱「英格蘭之獸」，並接受下一週的工作安排，然後不再進行辯論。

　　雪球被驅逐已經讓動物們驚惶失色，拿破崙的這番話更教他們大感鬱悶。如果知道怎麼反駁，有幾隻動物當下就會提出論點。像拳師，他為此感到大惑不解，耳朵向後貼平，抖了幾下額頭上的鬃毛，費力地想理出個頭緒，但最後仍想不出任何說詞。一些豬倒是口齒伶俐，四隻在前排的小肉豬尖聲反對，他們全跳起身來紛紛搶著發言。但突然間，圍坐在拿破崙身邊的那群狗發出一陣威脅的低聲咆哮，四隻小肉

豬只得再次坐下，緘口不言。接著，羊群的叫聲又響起來：
「四條腿是好漢，兩條腿是壞蛋！」持續了幾近十五鐘，在
這樣的氣氛下，大家根本已經無從討論了。

後來，史奎爾受命在農莊裡兜了一圈，就這個新的安排
向動物們解釋。

「同志們，」他說，「拿破崙同志將權責之外的工作往
自己身上攬，犧牲奉獻的精神，我相信農莊裡的每一隻動物
都心存感激。同志們，千萬不要以爲當領袖是一種享受！恰
恰相反，它意味著艱難而繁重的職責。沒有誰能比拿破崙同
志更堅信所有動物一律平等。他也確實很想讓大家爲自己作
主，可是萬一你們失策了，同志們，那會怎樣呢？現在我們
知道雪球還不如一名罪犯，要是你們眞的跟從了他那荒誕無
稽的風車夢，現在的農莊又會是怎樣呢？」

「可他在『牛棚之役』表現得很勇敢。」有隻動物忍不
住說了一句。

「單有勇敢是不夠的，」史奎爾說，「忠誠和服從更爲
重要。就『牛棚之役』而言，我相信我們最終會有一天發現
雪球的功勞言過其實。紀律，同志們，如鐵般的紀律！這才
是我們今日的口號。一步走錯，我們的仇敵便會來顛覆我
們。同志們，你們肯定不想讓瓊斯再回來吧？」

又是一番無可辯駁的論點。毫無疑問，動物們當然不希望再看到瓊斯。如果辯論有可能導致他回來，那麼就應該取消辯論。拳師細細琢磨了好一陣子，終於能將自己的看法說出口：「如果這是拿破崙同志說的，那就一定沒錯。」如此一來，他的座右銘：「我會更加努力工作」的後面又加上了一句：「拿破崙同志永遠正確。」

到了季節更迭，春耕開始的時候，雪球的那間設計室還一直被封著，大家猜想著那些設計圖肯定早已從地板上被抹掉了。每個星期天的早晨十點鐘，動物們照例聚集在穀倉，接收一週的工作指令。大豬梅傑的頭顱已剩白骨，動物們將其從墓穴裡挖出來，放在旗杆下的一個木墩上，就在那把槍的旁邊。升旗之後，動物們要按規定恭恭敬敬地列隊經過那個顱骨，然後才能進入穀倉。近來，大家沒有再像先前那樣坐在一起過了。拿破崙、史奎爾和一頭名叫繆斯的豬一同坐在平臺的前緣。這位繆斯可是天賦非凡，善於吟詩譜曲。而九條狗以他們為中心圍坐成半圓，其他的豬坐在後方，其他的動物們則是坐在穀倉中央面向他們。拿破崙像發表軍令般一板一眼地宣讀一週的工作安排，隨後，只是唱了一遍「英格蘭之獸」，就解散全體動物們。

雪球被逐後的第三個星期天，拿破崙竟然宣布要建造風車。動物們聽到這個消息終究是有些吃驚，而拿破崙也沒有說明他改變心意的原因，只是簡單地告誡動物們，建造風車

的任務將非常艱苦——有必要的話，會因此縮減大家的口糧。慶幸的是，建造計畫已規劃完畢，就連細節的部份也面面俱到，特別委員會過去三週都爲了這個計畫忙碌著。建造風車，加上各種改善工程，預期要花費兩年時間。

當天晚上，史奎爾私底下對其他動物一一解釋，說拿破崙從來沒有眞正反對過建造風車。相反地，整個風車專案的構想是他先提出的。雪球畫在孵蛋室地上的那份設計圖，實際上是他早些時候從拿破崙的筆記中剽竊的。事實上，風車完全是拿破崙的獨創。有動物問道，那當初爲什麼拿破崙要強烈反對呢？這時史奎爾一臉狡詐，他說，這正是拿破崙同志的老練之處，他裝作反對風車，那只是一個計謀，目的在於驅除雪球這個隱患，這個十惡不赦的壞東西。既然現在雪球已經溜掉了，計畫就能在沒有雪球妨礙的情況下順利進行了。史奎爾說，這就是所謂的策略。「策略，同志們，策略！」他重複了好幾遍，他一邊歡快地笑著，一邊甩動著尾巴躑來躑去。動物們一時還不太明白這個詞的意思，可是史奎爾的話很有說服力，加上剛巧有三條氣勢洶洶的狗在他身邊低吼，大家也就沒有再問下去，接受了他的解釋。

第 6 章

　　整整一年，動物們像奴隸一樣地終日勞作。但好在他們樂在其中，無論流血還是流汗都心甘情願、毫無怨言。他們知道：雖然辛苦，但在這裡所付出的一點一滴都是真正地為了自己和後代子孫，而不再是為了那幫遊手好閒、寄生成性的人類。

　　從初春到夏末，他們每周都要工作六十個小時。八月，拿破崙又規定了星期天下午也不能休息。理論上，這一段時間的工作與否完全出於大家的自願，不過，無論是誰，凡是缺勤的都要被減去一半的口糧。但即使算上加班，大家還是發覺有些活根本就是幹不完的。今年的收穫是略遜於去年的，而且，因為耕作沒有及早完成，本來該在初夏就播種番薯的兩塊地至今顆粒無收。冬天該怎樣生活呢？大家籠罩在一片灰濛濛的悲觀預想中。

　　風車的事引發了一連串意外的難題。按說，農莊裡本就有一個質地很好的石灰岩採石場，動物們又在一間小屋裡發

現了大量的沙子和水泥，所有的建築材料就這樣極其順利
地齊備了。但問題是，誰也沒有砌石和建築的經驗，雖然
面對大量石料卻一個個全都手足無措。十字鎬和撬棍看來
是必要的工具，可是，動物們誰也不會用後腿站立，也就
無法使用這些只適合於人類生理特點的工具。在他們徒勞
了幾個星期之後，不知是誰想出了一個利用重力作用的辦
法。採石場上到處都是巨大的圓石，大家用繩子綁住這些
圓石，再由牛、馬、羊和所有能抓住繩子的動物合力 ——
甚至豬有時也在關鍵時刻搭把手 —— 拖著石頭，慢慢地沿
著斜坡拖到礦頂。到了那兒，再把石頭從邊上堆下去摔成
碎塊。這樣一來，運輸的工作倒顯得相對簡單
一些了。馬用貨車拉，羊零碎地拖運，就
連穆勒和班傑明也套上了一輛破舊的
兩輪座車，盡了他們微薄的心
力。就這樣到了夏末，石料
便積累充足了。接著，
在豬的監督下，風
車工程終於正
式啟動。

　　不幸的是，整個採石的過程一直進展緩慢。僅僅把一塊圓石拖到礦頂，常常就要竭盡全力地幹上整整一天。還有些時候，石頭雖然被順利地從礦頂推了下去，卻毫髮無損。多虧拳師發揮了超常的作用，要沒有他那身萬夫不擋的蠻力，恐怕什麼事都不會幹成。當圓石開始往下滑，拉石頭的動物因而被拖下山坡絕望哀叫時，拳師總是能及時趕到，拉住繩索，制止了一場迫在眉睫的悲劇。拳師的全力以赴與任勞任怨為他贏得了全體動物們衷心的欽佩和讚歎。克羅薇經常會過來叮囑他要多加小心，不要勞累過度傷了身體，但他從來不把這些放在心上。只是一如既往地用「我會更加努力工作」和「拿破崙同志永遠正確」這兩句口頭禪來回答所有的問題。他甚至和那隻報曉的小公雞商量好，把叫醒他的時間由原先的比大家提早半小時改為提早三刻鐘。同時，儘管日常的工作已把時間幾乎都占滿了，空閒時間裡，他仍獨自到採石場去，裝上一車碎石，在沒有任何幫助下悶頭向工地拉去。

　　儘管工作艱辛，大家這年夏天過得不算太糟，雖然他們能夠得到的口糧並不比瓊斯時代多多少，但比起那時來好歹也不能算少。關鍵在於，除了自己的食用之外，大家再也不必去供養那五隻寄生人類了。有了這至關重要的一點，其他的種種不足也就顯得微不足道了。另外，動物們的工作效率在這時也大有提高。比如鋤草這類活，動物們可以幹得完美

無缺，而人類卻永遠也做不到。再說，動物們也不再偷雞摸狗地行竊了，籬笆也因此而完成了它的歷史使命，大量的維護工作自然也完全可以省去。但儘管如此，夏季剛過，就有大量的各種各樣意想不到的困難一下子湧現出來：農莊裡需要煤油、釘子、線繩、狗食餅乾以及馬蹄上釘的鐵掌，但農莊裡無法生產這些東西。後來，又有了對種子和化肥的需求，還要有各類工具和風車零件。這些東西能從哪兒來呢？，誰也想不出個頭緒。

　　一個星期天的早晨，動物們照例集合起來準備接受新的指令。拿破崙忽然宣布，他已經決定執行一項新的政策，從現在起允許動物農莊同鄰近的農莊做些交易——這當然不含任何商業目的，而僅僅是為了獲得某些急需物資。他說，為了風車工程，我們要不惜一切代價。因此，他決定賣掉一些乾草和小麥，而且，如果還需要更多的錢，那就得賣雞蛋了，畢竟雞蛋在威靈頓一直是很搶手的。為風車工程所做的任何犧牲都將是她們最高的榮耀。

　　動物們再次感到一種說不出來的彆扭。「決不和人來往，決不從事交易，決不用錢」，這些早年的建園宣言不是早已經確立並且深入人心了嗎？那些信誓旦旦的情形至今都還歷歷在目——或者說至少他們認為自己還記得。那四隻曾在拿破崙宣布廢除大會議時提出過些許抗議的幼豬膽怯地準備發言，但一聽到狗的咆哮便很快閉上了嘴。接著，羊又照

例咩咩地叫起來：「四條腿是好漢，兩條腿是壞蛋！」一時的難堪場面也就算順利地對付過去了。最後，拿破崙抬起前蹄，平靜了一下氣氛，宣布說他已經安排好了一切，任何一隻動物都不必介入和人類打交道這項最為可鄙的事務中，作為領袖，他將把全部重擔都壓在自己肩上。一個住在威靈頓的名叫溫普爾的律師已經同意擔任動物農莊和外面社會的中間人，他將在每個星期一的早晨來訪接受拿破崙的指示。最後，拿破崙照例高呼一聲：「動物農莊萬歲！」結束了演說。動物們便齊聲高唱「英格蘭之獸」，會議就此散場。

會後的安撫工作是史奎爾不變的拿手好戲，他向大家打了包票，說反對從事交易和反對用錢的宣言從來沒有通過，搞不好連有關的提議都是子虛烏有的事。如果追溯謠言的根源，那就很可能是某一個來自雪球的陰謀詭計。對那些還是半信半疑的動物，史奎爾便厲聲問到：「你們分明是把夢裡的事和現實生活搞混了！同志們，你們見過這個宣言的記錄嗎？它寫在哪兒了？」自然，這類東西從來都沒有見諸文字過。因此，動物們便真的相信是他們自己搞錯了。

那個叫溫普爾的律師十分矮小，留著絡腮胡，看起來一臉奸詐。他的業務規模不大，但他本人卻足夠敏銳，早就看出了動物農莊會需要經紀人，而且傭金會相當可觀。按照協定，每個星期一溫普爾先生都要來農莊一趟。動物們對人類還是存留幾分畏懼，看著他來來去去，都避之惟恐不及。不

過，在他們這些四條腿的動物看來，拿破崙向著兩條腿的溫普爾發號施令的情景，激發了他們無比的自豪，這在一定程度上也讓他們感覺到這個新政策還是相當不錯的。現在，他們同人類的關係早已今非昔比。但是，人們對動物農莊的嫉恨不但沒有因為它的繁榮而有所消解，反而比以往更勝。而且每個人都堅信動物農莊的破產只是遲早的事。他們還在酒館的聚會裡，用充滿圖表的論證來說明那個風車注定要倒塌，即便它能建成，那也只是個無法運作的廢物。然而，儘管不情願，他們對動物們對農莊的管理能力也不由得刮目相看了。他們在稱呼動物農莊時，不再固執地沿用「曼諾農莊」這個名字，而是終於認可了動物們的叫法，用起了「動物農莊」這個原本是公認為離經叛道的名稱。所有人都放棄了對瓊斯先生的支援，而瓊斯先生自己也早已萬念俱灰，不再懷有任何復辟的希望，靜悄悄地移居到別的郡上了。如今，多虧了這個溫普爾，動物農莊才有了和外面的世界相接觸的機會。但小道消息總是不斷，說是拿破崙正準備同狐木農莊的皮爾金頓先生，或者是平徹菲爾德的弗雷德里克先生簽訂一項商業協定，不過，這個協定只會和兩家中的一家簽訂。

大約就是在這時，豬突然搬進了農莊主的院子，在那裡住下了。這一回，動物們又模糊地想起來，在早先的宣言裡有一條是反對這樣做的。史奎爾再度及時地說服大家事實並

非如此。他說，豬是農莊的首腦，一個安靜的工作場所是必要的，這樣才能保證各項決策工作的順利進行。再說，對於維護領袖（近來他在談到拿破崙的時侯，已經開始使用「領袖」這一尊稱）的尊嚴，一所潔淨的房屋是遠勝於一間豬圈的。儘管這樣，但在一聽到豬不但使用廚房來進行烹調，而且還佔用了客廳當作娛樂室，甚至睡在床上之後，還是有一些動物為此深感不安。只有拳師滿不在乎，淡淡地說了一句：「拿破崙同志永遠正確。」但是克羅薇卻堅持認為確實存在著一條反對使用床鋪的誡律。她跑到穀倉那裡，試圖從「七誡」當中找出答案。結果卻發現她自己已經把學業荒廢到連單個的字母都認不出來的程度。她只好找來穆勒。

「穆勒」她說，「妳來給我念一下第四條誡律，它是不是說了決不能睡在床上什麼的？」

穆勒費了好大的氣力才拼讀出來。

「它說，『任何動物不得睡在床鋪上使用床單』。」她可算念了出來。

奇怪的是，克羅薇從不記得第四條誡律提到過床單，可它既然就寫在牆上，那一定就是如此了。正巧，史奎爾在幾條狗的陪同下路過這裡，他從一個特殊的角度來解釋了整個問題。

「那麼，同志們，你們已經聽到我們這些豬睡到床上的事了？這又有什麼不好？你們就不想想，真的有過什麼誡律反對睡床嗎？床只不過是指代一個睡覺的地方，從這一點來說，窩棚裡的稻草堆就是一張床。這條誡律根本就是反對床單的，因為床單才是屬於人類的發明。我們已經把床上的床單全撤掉了，另外換上了幾條毛毯。這也足夠舒適了。可是同志們，我得告訴你們，我們的工作要消耗大量的腦力，和我們如此多的付出相比，這些東西並不見得有什麼過分。同志們，你們總不能不讓我們休息吧？你們一定也不願讓我們因為勞累過度而失職吧？更重要的是，你們之中有誰願意看到瓊斯那傢伙回來嗎？」

大家總算打消疑慮，而且也不再議論這件事了。幾天之後，聽到又有宣布說，今後豬的起床時間要比其他動物晚上一個小時，也就不再有誰對此抱怨什麼。

到了秋天，大家都累得不行了，好在心情尚佳。說起來他們已經在各種艱難困苦中熬足了整整一年，在賣掉了一些乾草和穀物之後，用來過冬的糧食就顯得不太充裕了，好在風車補償了這一切。工程已近一半了，秋收以後，是一連串秋高氣爽的日子，大家的幹勁因此而提高了不少。他們整天都在拖運石塊，奔忙不休。看著牆壁在一尺尺地加高，覺得自己的辛勤勞動實在是非常值得。拳師甚至在夜裡也不閒著，總愛藉著收穫月的月光再多幹上一兩個小時。大家的樂

趣就是在忙裡偷閒的時候繞著進行了一半的工程走來走去，讚歎著那牆壁的強度和近乎完美的垂直，讚歎著自己用數不清的汗水換來的成果，對一件如此偉大的工程能夠在自己的手裡完成而驚喜交加。唯獨老班傑明對風車毫無熱情，他如同往常一樣，除了不斷地重複著「驢都長壽」這句飽含玄機的名言之外，就再也無所表示了。

十一月到了，刮起了猛烈的西南風。一直多雨，沒辦法和水泥了，風車工程只得中斷。一天晚上，忽然間狂風大作，整個農莊都被撼動得搖晃，穀倉的頂棚瓦片翻飛。雞群同時在夢裡聽到了遠處有槍聲響起，突然驚醒，嘎嘎亂叫。

好不容易熬到早晨，動物們走出窩棚，發現旗杆已被風吹倒，果園邊上的一棵榆樹也被連根拔起。突然，動物們齊聲絕望地大叫，眼前是一幅糟透的場面——風車毀了。

大家一致衝向現場。一向沉著幹練的的拿破崙跑在最前頭。是的，他們的全部奮鬥成果倒在那兒了，只留下一地狼籍，他們好不容易弄碎又好不容易才運來的石塊散亂在四處。大家呆呆地望著這些碎石塊，心都碎了。拿破崙默默地踱著步子，偶爾爬在地面聞上一聞。他的尾巴僵直，不時左右抽動幾下，這正是他深思的表現。突然，他停住了，好像是拿定了主意。

「同志們，」他的聲調非常平和，「你們知道這是誰在做孽嗎？你們知道昨天晚上究竟是誰毀了我們風車？就是雪球！」他突然吼道：「這是雪球幹的！這個叛徒！這個居心叵測的傢伙！他摸黑爬到這兒，毀了我們近一年的辛勤勞動。是的，他妄圖阻撓我們偉大的計畫，為了他屈辱的被逐報復我們！同志們，我宣布對雪球判處死刑。並且，無論是誰，只要能夠抓到雪球，並能依據我的判決對他行刑，就將被授予『動物英雄』二級勳章和半蒲式耳的蘋果！活捉他將能得到整整一蒲式耳的蘋果！」

竟然是雪球犯下了如此的滔天大罪！動物們既驚愕又憤慨，便開始商量捉拿雪球的辦法。幾乎與此同時，在離小丘

不遠的草地上，發現了一行模糊的豬蹄印。雖然那些蹄印只能跟蹤出幾步遠，但看得出是朝著樹籬缺口的方向。拿破崙對著蹄印仔細地嗅了一番，然後一口咬定那一定就是雪球，並猜測雪球有可能是來自狐木農莊。

「別再猶豫了，同志們！」拿破崙又抬起了頭道：「還有工作在等著我們，我們要重建風車，而且就從今天早晨開始！在這個冬天之內我們定要完工！我們要投入全副精力，不管颳風下雨。我們要讓這個卑鄙的叛徒知道，我們的宏圖偉業是不會就這樣被輕易破壞掉的！記住，同志們，我們的計畫不僅不會有任何改變，反而更要一絲不苟地進行下去。前進吧，同志們！風車萬歲！動物農莊萬歲！」

第 7 章

　　這是一個寒冷的多天。彷彿永遠都不會停歇的狂風暴雨總算是過去了，但很快，天上又是雨雪交加。曠日的嚴寒直到二月才見和緩。動物們都在全力以赴地趕建風車，因為誰都清楚：外界的眼光從來就沒有離開過他們，如果風車沒有如期重建完成，那些兩眼冒火的人類定會為此幸災樂禍。

　　那些不懷好意的人類揚言他們根本就不相信風車會是被雪球破壞的。他們寧願相信風車的倒塌純粹是因為牆壁的厚度不夠。動物們雖然從來不這麼看，但還是決定築牆的厚度不能少於三英尺，而不是上一次的一英尺半。這也意味著採石工作量的成倍加重。但好長一段時間裡，採石場上都是不化的積雪，嚴重阻礙了工作的進行。後來，天氣漸漸轉為乾冷，才勉強開工了，但大家再也不像早先那樣滿懷希望、信心十足。總有難以驅散的冷意，總有難以壓制的飢餓感。只有拳師和克羅薇依然保持著當初的幹勁。史奎爾不時地來做一些華麗的演說，把勞動的樂趣與工作所帶來的神聖感闡述得淋漓盡致。但真正給大家鼓舞的卻是拳師那無與倫比的任

勞任怨和他時刻不離嘴邊的那句格言：「我會更加努力工作。」

　　一月份，開始出現了食物短缺。糧食配給急遽減少，上面的通知說要額外給大家發些馬鈴薯，可隨後卻發現由於地窖的遮蓋不夠嚴密，絕大部分的馬鈴薯都已經遭受了嚴重的凍傷，變得又軟又褪色，真正能吃的很少。這段日子裡，穀糠和蘿蔔成了大家唯一的食品，飢荒的事實近在眼前。對外遮掩這一實情已成了當務之急。因為風車的倒塌而壯了膽的人類更因此捏造出關於動物農莊的種種新奇的謊言。比如有謠傳說這裡所有的動物都在饑荒和疾病中垂死掙扎，並爆發了一次甚於一次的內訌，同類相食和吞食幼崽的慘境更是每天都在發生。拿破崙深知其中利害，便決意利用溫普爾先生的中立身份來做些闢謠。本來，溫普爾的每次來訪都很少與動物們接觸。但這次，拿破崙卻挑選了一些動物──大部分是羊，要他們在溫普爾能聽得到的地方，裝出一些無意的閒聊，內容都圍繞著口糧增加的主題。不僅如此，拿破崙又下令把儲藏室裡那些空箱子填滿沙土，再把僅存的一些糧食薄薄地蓋在上面，一切就緒之後，便找個適當的藉口，把溫普爾領到儲藏室去，不經意地讓他瞥上一眼。溫普爾就這樣被騙了過去，如拿破崙所願地在外界為糧食短缺問題大力闢謠。

　　然而，到了一月底，再不想辦法取得糧食，農莊顯然就

要崩潰了。這些天來，拿破崙不再輕易露面，整天地待在莊主的院子裡，那裡每一道門都由氣勢洶洶的狗把守著。一旦外出，總是頗具威儀，六條狗前呼後擁著，對任何走近的動物報以凶猛的吼叫。即使在星期天的早晨大家也常常見不到他，而總是由其他豬——通常是史奎爾——來發布他的最新指示。

在一個星期天的早晨，史奎爾鄭重宣布，從今以後，所有的母雞都必須把雞蛋上交。因為通過溫普爾的仲介，拿破崙已經簽了一份每周出售四百隻雞蛋的契約。這筆生意所賺的錢可以解決迫在眉睫的口糧短缺問題，農莊也就可以因此堅持到夏天。到了夏天，情況就會好轉了。

這項指示引起了雞群的強烈抗議。雖然此前她們已被警告過恐怕要做出必要的犧牲，但從不相信這種事真會發生。此時，母雞們剛剛備好的蛋是準備在春天孵化成小雞的，因而便抗議說，現在拿走雞蛋就等於謀財害命。於是，出於對自身基本權利的維護，她們在三隻年輕的黑米諾卡雞的帶動下，索性豁出去了。她們飛到椽子上下蛋，讓雞蛋落到地上摔得粉碎。這是農莊裡自瓊斯被逐之後的第一次帶有反叛意味的行動。對此，拿破崙立即採取了嚴厲措施。他指示停發雞的糧食配給，同時下令，哪怕是分給母雞們一丁點穀物都將被視為反叛並處以死刑。狗來負責具體的執法工作。堅持了五天之後，母雞們終於投降了。在這期間共有九隻雞死

去，遺體都埋到了果園，對外則宣稱他們是死於一場雞瘟。
溫普爾對此事毫不知情。雞蛋嚴格地按時交付，每周都有一
輛食品車來農莊裡驗貨取貨。

　　這段時間再也沒有出現雪球的蹤影。但關於他的傳聞始
終不斷。有的說他就躲在附近的農莊裡，不是在狐木農莊就
是在平徹菲爾德農莊。此時，拿破崙和其他農莊的關係也比
以前稍有改善。碰巧，在農莊的場院裡，有一堆已經堆了十
年的山毛櫸木料，已經風乾得徹底，於是溫普爾建議把它賣
掉。皮爾金頓先生和弗雷德里克先生願意出價，可拿破崙還
在猶豫應該賣給誰比較好。大家注意到，每當他似乎要和弗
雷德里克達成協定的時候，就有謠傳說雪球正躲在狐木農
莊；而當他轉而傾向皮爾金頓時，就又有謠傳說雪球正躲是
在平徹菲爾德。

　　初春時節，突然有一件事震驚了整個農莊。不知從哪裡
傳來的消息，說雪球常在夜間祕密地潛入！動物們全都嚇壞
了，躲在窩棚裡夜不能寐。據說，每天晚上他都在夜幕的掩
護下偷偷地溜進來，蓄意報復，無惡不作。他偷走穀子，弄
翻牛奶桶，打碎雞蛋，踐踏苗圃，咬掉果樹皮。不論是什麼
時候，不論是什麼事情搞砸了，都會被歸咎到雪球身上，要
是一扇窗戶壞了或者下水道堵了，一定會有誰斷定這是雪球
在夜間幹的。儲藏室的鑰匙丟了，大家都堅信是雪球給扔到
井裡去了。但奇怪的是，等到終於發現鑰匙原來是被錯放在

一袋麵粉底下之後，他們依然對雪球的罪惡堅信不移。奶牛異口同聲地稱雪球在她們睡覺時溜進牛棚，偷喝了她們的奶。那些在多天曾給大家帶來無盡煩惱的老鼠，也被指責為雪球的同夥。

有鑒於此，拿破崙下令對雪球的行蹤進行一次全面調查。他在狗的護衛下親自來做這項工作，其他動物全都謙恭地尾隨在後。每走幾步，拿破崙就要停下來，嗅一嗅地面上是否有雪球的氣味 —— 他聲稱自己能辨別。他嗅遍了每一個角落，從穀倉、牛棚到雞窩和蘋果園，幾乎到處都發現了雪球的蹤跡。每到一處，他就把嘴伸到地上，深深地吸上幾下，隨即驚異地大叫道：「雪球！他到過這兒！我聞得出來！」一聽到「雪球」這兩個字，所有的狗都一齊呲牙裂嘴，發出一陣令大家膽顫心驚的咆哮。

大家全被嚇壞了。對他們來說，雪球就像某種隱身的惡魔，無聲無息地出沒在他們的周圍，伺機對動物們造成威脅。到了晚上，史奎爾把大家召集起來，惶惶恐恐地宣告嚴重消息。

「同志們！我們發現了一件最可怕的事情，雪球已經向平徹菲爾德農莊的弗雷德里克賣身投靠。而弗雷德里克那傢伙正在計畫著襲擊我們，妄圖霸佔我們的農莊！當他們發動攻擊，雪球將作為他的指引出賣我們大家。更糟的是，我們一向以為，雪球的反叛僅僅是出於驕傲和野心。可我們錯

了，同志們，你們知道他眞正的動機是什麼嗎？雪球打從一開始就和瓊斯是一夥的！他自始至終都是瓊斯的密探。我們剛剛發現了一些他丟下的文件，這才證實了這個實在令人難以置信的事實！同志們，依我看，這就能解釋很多的問題了。在牛棚之役中，雖然幸虧他的陰謀沒有得逞，但他想毀滅我們的企圖難道不是昭然若揭嗎？」

大家都愣住了。比起破壞風車的那樁事，這項罪名可要嚴重得太多了。但大家實在難以接受這一事實。他們都還記得──或者說他們認爲自己記得，在牛棚之役中，雪球英勇地帶領大家衝鋒陷陣是有目共睹的，即使瓊斯的子彈已射進它的脊背他也毫不退縮。一開始大家難以把瓊斯同夥的身分聯想到雪球身上，就連拳師也搞不懂了。他臥在地上，前腿彎在身子底下，眼睛緊閉著，絞盡腦汁想釐清思路。

「我不相信，」他說道，「雪球在牛棚之役中奮勇作戰，這是我親眼看到的。戰鬥一結束，我們不是就立刻授予他『動物英雄』一級勳章了嗎？」

「那是我們的失誤。同志，因爲我們現在才知道，他實際上是想引誘我們走向全軍覆滅。在我們已發現的祕密文件當中，這一點寫得清清楚楚。」

「但他的確是負傷了，」拳師說，「我們都看見他一邊流血一邊衝鋒陷陣。」

「那也是他陰謀中的一部分！」史奎爾叫道，「瓊斯的子彈只不過擦了一下他的皮。要是你能識字的話，我會把他自己寫的文件拿給你看。他們的陰謀，就是要在關鍵時刻發出一個信號，讓雪球逃跑並把農莊留給人類。他幾乎就要成功了，我甚至敢說，要是沒有我們英勇的領袖拿破崙同志，他的奸計早就得逞了。難道你們不記得了，就在瓊斯一夥衝進院子的時候，雪球突然轉身就逃，很多動物跟著他就跑？還有，就在那一會兒，大家全陷入了慌亂，幾乎就要完蛋了，是拿破崙同志突然衝上前去，大喊：『消滅人類！』同時一口咬住了瓊斯的腿，難道你們不記得了嗎？你們肯定記得！」史奎爾一邊左蹦右跳，一邊大聲叫喊。

既然史奎爾把那副場景描述得如此逼真，大家便相信是確有其事了。不管怎麼說，他們記得在激戰的關鍵時刻，雪球的確曾經掉頭逃過。但是拳師還是有些疑惑。

他慢吞吞地說：「我還是不能相信雪球一開始就是一個叛徒。他後來的所作所為是另一回事，但我認為在牛棚之役中，他是一個好同志。」

「我們的領袖，拿破崙同志，」史奎爾以緩慢而堅定的語氣宣告，「已經明確地——明確地，同志們——聲明雪球一開始就是瓊斯的奸細，是的，遠在籌劃起義之前他就是奸細。」

「噢,這就不一樣了!如果這是拿破崙同志說的,那就肯定不會錯。」拳師說。

「這就是事實的真相,同志們!」史奎爾大叫著。但動物們注意到他那閃亮的小眼睛向拳師怪模怪樣地瞥了一下。他轉身要走,忽然停下來又強調了一句:「我提醒農莊裡的每個動物,你們要睜大眼睛。我們有理由相信,眼下,雪球的密探正潛伏在我們中間!」

四天以後的一個下午,拿破崙召集所有的動物在院子裡開會。在集合完畢之後,拿破崙威嚴地從屋裡出來了,佩戴著他的兩枚勳章(他最近已授予自己一枚「動物英雄」一級

勳章和一枚「動物英雄」二級勳章），還帶著他那九條大狗。那些狗圍著他蹦來蹦去，發出讓所有動物都毛骨悚然的吼叫。大家默默地蜷縮在那裡，似乎有了些不祥的預感。

拿破崙嚴厲地站在那兒，朝大家審視一番，接著便發出一聲尖細的驚叫。於是，那些狗立刻衝上前去，咬住了四頭小豬的耳朵，把他們往外拖。那四頭小豬在疼痛和恐懼中嚎叫著被拖到拿破崙腳下，耳朵流出血來。狗嘗到了血腥味，發狂了好一會兒。更讓大家吃驚的是，有三條狗竟然向拳師撲了過去。拳師看到他們撲來，不慌不忙地伸出巨掌，在半空中踢翻一條狗，又把他踩在腳上。那條狗發出了尖利的叫聲，慌忙求饒，另外的兩條狗見狀不對，夾著尾巴飛奔回來。拳師不解地看著拿破崙，不知道是該把那狗踩死呢還是放掉。拿破崙變了臉色，對拳師厲聲喝斥。拳師便抬起腳掌，讓那條狗帶著傷在哀號中溜走了。

喧囂立即平靜下來。那四頭小豬渾身發抖地等待發落，臉上寫著罪惡感。他們正是曾公開抗議拿破崙廢除星期天大會的那四頭小豬。接著，拿破崙喝令他們坦白罪行。沒等旁人催促，他們沒頭沒尾地交代說，自己從雪球被驅逐以後一直和他保持著祕密聯絡，在搗毀風車的罪行中也有他們的配合，並且還和雪球達成一項協定，打算把動物農莊拱手讓給弗雷德里克先生。他們還補充說雪球曾在私下裡對他們透露過，他過去幾年來一直都是瓊斯的間諜。招認剛剛結束，他

們的喉嚨就被狗的利齒咬穿了。

行刑完畢，拿破崙聲色俱厲地質問還有誰要坦白什麼。在這種恐怖氣氛的壓迫下，那三隻曾經在雞蛋事件中領頭鬧事的雞戰戰兢兢地走了上去，說雪球曾托夢給她們，煽動她們違抗拿破崙的命令。坦白完畢，她們也沒逃過被殺掉的命運。接著上來的是一隻鵝，說他曾在去年的收穫季節私藏了六穗穀子，並在當天晚上吃掉了。一隻羊也坦白說她曾向飲水池裡撒過尿，但這是雪球慫恿她這麼幹的。另外兩隻羊交待道，他們曾經謀殺了一隻老公羊，那是一隻十分忠實的拿破崙的信徒，他們在他正患咳嗽時，追著他圍著火堆轉來轉去。這些動物都被當場處以死刑。招認和行刑持續著，直到拿破崙的腳前已經屍體成堆，空氣中彌漫著濃重的血腥味，自從瓊斯被驅逐後再沒看過這樣的場面。

等一切都過去，豬狗以外的動物，便都擠成一堆溜走了。他們既驚又懼，但卻說不清到底什麼更使他們害怕——是那些和雪球結成同盟的叛逆更可怕呢，還是剛剛目睹的這些殘忍懲罰更可怕？過去，類似的流血場景也時常可見，但遠不如這次來得陰森恐怖，因為這就發生在他們自己同志之間。從瓊斯逃離農莊直到現在，還從沒有發生過動物之間相互殘殺的慘劇，就連老鼠也未曾受過傷害。這時，大家已經走到小丘上，尚未完工的風車孤零零地矗立在那裡。他們躺在一起互相取暖，克羅薇、穆勒、班傑明、牛、羊，鵝群和

雞群，除了貓之外全都在這兒了，而貓在集合的時候就已經失蹤了。一時間沒任何動物說話，只有拳師還站著，一邊煩躁不安地走動，一邊用尾巴不斷地在身上抽打，間或驚訝地嘶鳴，最後，他終於說話了：

「我不明白，我真不願相信這種事會發生在我們的農莊裡，這一定是我們做錯了什麼。如果說有什麼補救辦法，我想關鍵就是要更加努力地工作。從今天起，早上我要再提前一個小時起床。」

他步履沉重地走開了，走向了採石場。一到那兒，便連續採了兩車石頭，直拉到風車的建設基地，忙到晚上才收工回去。

大家都擠在克羅薇的周圍默默不語。在他們躺著的地方有著遼闊的視野，可以俯視幾乎整個村莊。狹長的牧場伸向那條大路，耕地裡長著碧綠的麥苗，還有草地、樹叢、池塘，還有農莊裡的紅色屋頂和那煙囪裡冒出的嫋嫋輕煙。這是一個春天的傍晚，夕陽的餘暉灑在青草地和茂盛的叢林之上，蕩漾著片片金輝。他們忽然意識到，這是他們自己的農莊，每一寸土地都歸他們自己所有，他們為此驚訝，在此之前，他們從未發現這裡竟是如此美麗，如此令他們心馳神往。克羅薇已經止不住奪眶而出的熱淚。如果她有辦法能夠說出此時的想法，她肯定會說：我們已經背離了當年為推翻

人類而許下的諾言，這些殘酷的殺戮並不是我們在大豬梅傑鼓動起義的那天晚上所嚮往的。對於未來，如果說她還曾有過什麼設想，那一定是這樣的一個社會——在那裡，沒有飢餓，沒有鞭子，一切平等，大家各盡所能，強者保護弱者——就像在大豬梅傑講演的那天晚上，她曾經彎曲著前腿保護著那一群遲到的小鴨子一樣。

但她不明白，當那些氣勢洶洶的狗到處咆哮的時候、當眼看著自己的同志在坦白了可怕的罪行後被撕成碎片的時候，為什麼沒人膽敢說出內心真實的想法。

她的心裡沒有反叛或者違命的念頭。她知道，儘管如此，他們現在的處境也已遠勝於瓊斯時代了，當務之急還是要防備人類的捲土重來。不管發生了什麼事，她始終會保持忠心耿耿，辛勤勞動，服從拿破崙的領導，完成他交給自己的一切任務。但她仍然相信，她和其他的動物們曾滿懷期望並為之不懈奮鬥的，並不是今天的這般場景；他們建造風車，勇敢地冒著瓊斯一夥的槍林彈雨衝鋒陷陣也不是為了將來會落得這般結果。這就是她此刻的深切感受，雖然她貧乏的詞彙無法表達。

最後她發現有一種方法能代替言語，便張開了喉嚨，低低地唱起了「英格蘭之獸」。這曲調忽然有了異乎尋常的感染力，漸漸地，愈來愈多的聲音加入了這支旋律，一遍又一

遍，和諧卻緩慢，低沉卻淒然。這是第一次，第一次大家以這樣的心態、這樣的嗓音唱起這首不能再熟悉的歌曲，別有一番滋味湧上了心頭。

就在他們第三遍唱起歌時，歌聲卻被史奎爾打斷了。他在兩條狗的陪同下，宣布了拿破崙同志的一項特別命令──「英格蘭之獸」已被廢止。從今以後這首歌列為禁唱曲目。

大家怔住了。

「為什麼？」穆勒嚷道。

「不再需要了，同志們，」史奎爾冷冷地說，『英格蘭之獸』是革命歌曲。但革命已經成功，今天下午對叛徒的處決就是整個革命的最後行動。另外，內外部的敵人已經全部被打垮了。我們在『英格蘭之獸』中所表達的是在當時對未來美好社會的渴望，但這個社會現在已經建立起來。這首歌顯然已不再有任何意義了。」

大家感到一種莫名的恐懼，有些動物正要抗議的時候，羊群大聲地咩咩叫起那套老調子來：「四條腿是好漢，兩條腿是壞蛋。」一直叫嚷了好幾分鐘，也就淹沒了這場爭議。

於是，「英格蘭之獸」再也聽不到了，取而代之的，是豬中的才子繆斯寫的另外一首歌曲，它是這樣開頭的：

動物農莊，動物農莊，

吾輩誓不讓汝受損罹傷！

從此，每個星期天早晨的升旗之後就改唱這首歌了。但對大家來說，無論歌詞還是曲調，這首繆斯的作品遠不能和「英格蘭之獸」相提並論。

第 8 章

　　幾天以後，行刑造成的恐慌已經平息下來，一些動物這才想起了第六條誡律中彷彿有過這樣一條規定：「任何動物都不得傷害同類。」在討論這個話題時，大家總是儘量地避開那些豬狗，他們隱約覺得這次殺戮與第六誡律是有衝突的。克羅薇請求班傑明給她念一下第六誡律，而班傑明像往常一樣地寧可置身事外。最後還是穆勒給她念了：「任何動物不得無緣無故地傷害同類。」莫名地，「無緣無故」這幾個字，動物們幾乎沒有任何印象。但他們明白了對叛徒的制裁並不是毫無理由的，當年的誡律並沒有被違反。

　　這一年，動物們比前些年更加辛苦。重建風車，不但要把牆築得有上一次的兩倍那麼厚，還有著緊迫的時間期限，再加上農莊的例行性勞動，工作量是相當驚人的。大家發現，現在的勞作時間已明顯地長於瓊斯時代了，伙食卻並不比那時候好。每到星期天早上，史奎爾的蹄子上就捏著一張長紙條，向大家公布各類食物產量增加的一系列資料，根據內容分門別類，有的增加了百分之二百，有的增加了百分之

三百或者百分之五百。動物們覺得沒有任何理由不相信他，尤其是因爲他們再也記不清楚起義前的情形到底是什麼樣了。不過，他們常常是寧願數字少些而食物多些。

現在，所有的命令都是通過史奎爾或是另一頭豬發布的，拿破崙自己兩星期也難得露一次面。一旦他要出現在公開場合，那就不僅有狗侍衛的前呼後擁，而且還有一隻黑色的小公雞鳴鑼開道：在拿破崙講話之前，小公雞先要響亮地啼叫一下。據說，即使在莊主的院子裡，拿破崙也是和別的豬分開住的，用餐要由兩條狗伺候著，食具用的是曾在客廳玻璃碗櫃裡的上好瓷器。另外，每逢拿破崙的生日也要鳴槍致敬了，就像其他的兩個紀念日一樣。稱呼上也作了改變，直呼其名是大不敬的，而要稱呼：「偉大的領袖拿破崙同志」，而那些豬還喜歡錦上添花地給他冠以各式各樣的頭銜，如「動物之父」，「人類剋星」，「羊的保護神」，「鴨子的朋友」等等。史奎爾每次演講時，總要淚流滿面地大談一番拿破崙的無上智慧和慈悲心腸，說他對普天之下的動物，尤其是對那些還不幸地生活在其他農莊裡的受歧視和受奴役的動物，滿懷著深摯的愛。在農莊裡，大家已習慣於把遇到的每一件幸運和取得的每一項榮譽都歸功於偉大的拿破崙。你會常常聽到一隻雞對另一隻雞這樣講：「在偉大領袖拿破崙的指引下，我在六天之內下了五隻蛋」，或者兩頭正在飲水的牛高聲讚美：「多虧偉大領袖拿破崙同志的領

導，這水喝起來真甜！」農莊裡，動物們的整個精神狀態充
分體現在一首名爲「拿破崙同志」的詩中，詩是繆斯寫的，
才思泉湧：

孤兒的好友！

幸福的源頭！

哦，主，是您賜給了我們糧食！

您的雙眼堅毅沉著，

讓我總是有激情如火，

讓我總是有仰望的狂熱，

偉大的拿破崙同志！

每日的兩餐飽飯，

每夜那潔淨的草墊，

恩主呀，都歸功於您無私的賞賜！

每隻動物都能享有安睡，

連夢都做得很美，

都是因爲有了您的撫慰，

偉大的拿破崙同志！

> 我要是有頭幼崽，
> 幼小得惹人憐愛，
> 哪怕他還太小，還不太懂事，
> 他也應該學會
> 忠誠地聆聽您的教誨，
> 第一聲一定要這樣叫，我的寶貝：
> 「偉大的拿破崙同志！」

　　拿破崙對這首詩非常滿意，讓手下把它刻在穀倉的牆上，就在與「七誡」相對的另一頭。詩的上方是史奎爾用白漆完成的拿破崙的一幅側面畫像。

　　在這期間，由溫普爾牽線，拿破崙正著手與弗雷德里克及皮爾金頓就那堆待售的木材進行繁冗的談判。在這兩個人中，弗雷德里克更急著要買，但又不肯出一個公道的價錢。與此同時，有一個過去的謠言重新開始流傳，說弗雷德里克和他的夥計們正在密謀襲擊動物農莊，並想把那個他嫉恨已久的風車毀掉，而雪球也仍藏身在平徹菲爾德農莊。仲夏時節，大家又驚訝地聽說，另外有三隻雞也坦白交待了罪行，說他們曾受雪球的煽動，參與過一起刺殺拿破崙的陰謀。那三隻雞被立即處決了，而有鑒於此，為了拿破崙的安全，戒備措施更加完善。夜間，拿破崙的四個床腳都有一條狗作為

守衛，枕戈待旦：一頭名叫平克埃的豬在拿破崙吃飯之前嘗遍他的所有食物，以防有人下毒。

差不多同時，有消息說拿破崙決定把那堆木材賣給皮爾金頓先生；他還擬訂了一項關於動物農莊和狐木農莊之間以物易物的長期協定。儘管還是通過溫普爾牽線，但拿破崙和皮爾金頓先生現在的關係可以說是相當不錯的。對於皮爾金頓這個人，動物們並不信任。但他們更不信任弗雷德里克，那是個讓動物們又怕又恨的傢伙。夏天過去了，風車即將竣工，那個關於弗雷德里克將要襲擊農莊的風聲也愈來愈緊。凶險的戰鬥已經迫在眉睫，而且，據說弗雷德里克帶了人手二十，全都配有槍枝，還聽說他已經買通了地方官和警察，這樣，一旦他能把動物農莊的地契弄到手，就可以成為合法的所有人了。更有甚者，從平徹菲爾德農莊傳出了許多可怕的消息，說弗雷德里克正用他自己農莊裡的動物做些殘酷得令人髮指的演習。他用鞭子抽死了一匹老馬，餓他的牛，還把一條狗扔到爐子裡燒死了，到了晚上，他就把剃鬚刀的碎片綁在雞爪子上看鬥雞取樂。聽到這些消息，動物們群情激憤，熱血沸騰，他們不時叫嚷著要一起去進攻平徹菲爾德農莊，趕走那裡的人類，解放那裡的動物。他們之所以把火氣暫時壓了下來，是因為史奎爾一再告誡大家，要避免草率行動，要相信拿破崙的戰略布署。

儘管如此，反對弗雷德里克的情緒還是愈來愈高漲。在

一個星期天的早上，拿破崙來到穀倉，他解釋說他從來沒打算把那堆木料賣給弗雷德里克。他說，和那個惡棍打交道實在有辱他的身份。作為革命宣傳員的鴿子，以後將不准在狐木農莊落腳。他還下令，把他們過去的口號「打倒人類」換成「打倒弗雷德里克」。夏末，雪球的另一個陰謀又被揭露了。麥田裡之所以長滿雜草，原來是他曾在某個夜晚潛入農莊，往糧種裡拌了草籽。一隻與此事件有牽連的雄鵝向史奎爾坦白了這一罪行後就吞食了劇毒顛茄畏罪自殺了。大家還被告知，事實並不像他們一直認為的那樣：雪球從來都沒有受到過「動物英雄」一級勳章的嘉獎。受獎的事只不過是在牛棚之役後，由雪球自己散布的一個謊話。事實上，根本就沒有給他授勳這回事，倒是因為他在戰鬥中表現怯懦而早就受盡了譴責。這種解釋的確不是人人都能夠輕易接受的，但史奎爾的如簧之舌很快就使他們把這些都歸咎於自己遲鈍的記憶力。

到了秋天，大家竭盡全力，在不耽誤收割的前提下終於使風車竣工了。接下來的事就是安裝機器。溫普爾正在為購買機器的事到處交涉，但不管怎樣，風車的主體總算是完成了——不辭辛勞地，不管他們的經驗多麼不足，工具多麼原始，運氣多麼不佳，雪球的詭計多麼陰險，整個工程到此總算是在計畫之內如期完成了！驕傲遠遠壓過了超載的疲憊，他們繞著自己的這一傑作轉個不停。在他們眼裡，風車要比

第一次做得漂亮多了，另外，牆座也比第一次的厚了整整兩倍。除了炸藥，它堅固的身體已經能夠抵禦任何侵襲！回想當初為此付出的勞動、期間克服的沮喪，和風車的翼板帶動了發電機時，他們的生活因而會發生的巨大改變，他們就忘記了疲勞，發出勝利的歡呼。拿破崙在狗和公雞的前呼後擁下，親自視察，並親自對大家的豐功偉績表示祝賀，還鄭重地以「拿破崙」三個字為風車命名。

兩天後，大家被召集到穀倉，召開一次特別會議。拿破崙宣布，他已經把那堆木材賣給了弗雷德里克，明天就是交貨的日子。頓時，大家一個個都驚得目瞪口呆。原來，拿破崙與皮爾金頓之間只是一些表面工夫，實際上他已和弗雷德里克達成了祕密協定。

與狐木農莊的關係完全破裂了，他們去信向皮爾金頓發出了極盡能事的謾罵與侮辱，通知鴿子們要視平徹菲爾德農莊為禁地，還把「打倒弗雷德里克」的口號改成了「打倒皮爾金頓」。同時，拿破崙親自出面進行闢謠，所謂動物農莊面臨襲擊的說法是徹頭徹尾的謊言，弗雷德里克虐待動物的傳聞也純屬無稽之談。所有的謠言都很有可能是來自雪球及其同夥。總之，現在看來，雪球非但沒有藏在平徹菲爾德農莊，而且一直是住在狐木農莊裡面。作為皮爾金頓的最得力的跟班，每天享受著奢靡與腐化的生活。

　　拿破崙精明的算計使群豬欣喜若狂。與皮爾金頓的表面友好迫使弗雷德里克把價錢提高了十二英鎊。史奎爾說，拿破崙思想上的卓越之處，實際上就體現在他對任何人都不信任上，即使對弗雷德里克也是如此。弗雷德里克曾打算用一種叫做支票的東西支付木料錢，那玩意兒差不多只是一張白紙，只不過寫著保證支付之類的許諾而已，但拿破崙根本不是他能糊弄得了的，他要求用真正的五英鎊票子付款，而且還要款項收到後才供貨。這筆錢弗雷德里克已經如數付清，其數額剛好夠為風車添置機械。

　　木料很快就被拉走了，貨車剛剛離開，拿破崙便迫不及待地在穀倉裡又召開了一次特別會議，內容是讓動物們觀看弗雷德里克付給的鈔票。拿破崙笑逐顏開，心花怒放，他戴著他的兩枚勳章，端坐在演講台的草蓆上，錢就在他身邊整齊地堆放在廚房找來的瓷盤上。動物們排成一行慢慢走過，無不大飽眼福。拳師還伸出鼻子嗅了嗅那鈔票。

　　三天以後，在一陣嘈雜聲中，只見溫普爾飛車趕到，面如死灰。他把自行車就地一扔，徑直衝了進去農舍莊主的院子。很快，就在拿破崙的房間裡響起了一陣哽噎著嗓子的怒吼。出事了！這消息野火般迅速傳遍整個農莊──鈔票是假的！弗雷德里克白白地拉走了木料！

　　拿破崙立即把所有動物召集在一起，咬牙切齒地當眾判

處弗雷德里克死刑。他說，要是抓住這傢伙，非要把他活活煮死不可。同時他還告誡大家，繼這個背信棄義的行動之後，更糟糕的事情也就會一觸即發了。弗雷德里克和他的同夥隨時都可能發動他們蓄謀已久的襲擊。因此，馬上得在所有通向農莊的路口設置崗哨。另外，派四隻鴿子給狐木農莊去信安撫，希望能和皮爾金頓先生重歸於好。

但襲擊就在第二天的早晨突然開始了。當時正是早飯時間，哨兵飛報，說弗雷德里克已經來勢洶洶地逼近了大門。動物們懷著滿腔的怒火，立刻給敵人以迎頭痛擊，但這一回可不比「牛棚之役」能輕易取得勝利了。敵方有十五個人，六支槍，可怕的槍聲和惡毒的子彈已不是動物們的血肉之軀可以抵擋。雖然拿破崙和拳師不斷集結著攻勢，但始終不能衝進敵人的五十碼之內。隨著傷員的增多，大家對戰鬥開始絕望，於是四散奔逃，各自尋找藏身之地。不一會兒，整個牧場，還有風車，都已落入了敵手。拿破崙也已不知所措了，他一言不發地踱著步，尾巴變得僵硬，不停地抽搐著。他不時朝著狐木農莊的方向投去渴望的眼光。如果皮爾金頓的人能幫他們一把的話，這場戰鬥還不是沒有機會。但雪上加霜的是，前一天派出的四隻鴿子飛回來了，其中有一隻帶著皮爾金頓寫下的一張小紙片：「你們活該。」

這時，弗雷德里克一夥人已停在風車周圍。動物們一邊窺視著他們，一邊不安地嘀咕起來。有兩個人拿出一根鐵鍬

和一把大鐵錘：他們竟然要拆掉風車！

「這不可能！」拿破崙喊道，「我們已把牆築得那麼厚實，他們休想在一個星期之內拆掉它。不要怕，同志們！」

但班傑明仍在急切地注視著那些人的活動。拿著鐵鍬和大鐵錘的兩個人正在風車的地基附近打孔。終於，班傑明帶著幾乎是戲謔的神情，慢騰騰地呶了呶他那長長的嘴巴。

「我看出點眉目了，」他說，「過一會兒，他們就要往打好的孔裡裝填炸藥。」

動物們驚恐地等待著，現在冒險衝出掩蔽的建築是不可能的。果然，幾分鐘之後，眼看著那些人朝四下散開，接著，響起了震耳欲聾的爆炸聲。頓時，鴿子們飛到空中，其他動物（除了拿破崙外）全都轉過臉去，猛地趴倒在地。當他們起來後，只看到風車所在地上空飄蕩著一團巨大的黑色煙雲。煙消雲散之後，風車已灰飛煙滅！

此景之下動物們紛紛恢復了勇氣，片刻之前的膽怯和絕望，猛然間便被這卑鄙行為所激起的狂怒淹沒了。他們發出一陣強烈的復仇吶喊，不等進一步指令，便一齊向敵人衝去。這一次，他們顧不上留意那如冰雹一般掃射而來的子彈了。這是一場殘酷、激烈的戰鬥。那幫人不斷地開槍，等到動物們接近他們時，他們就掄起棍棒抬起厚靴大打出手。一

頭牛、三隻羊、兩隻鵝就這樣死在他們的手裡。每隻動物都
受了傷，就連一直在後面指揮作戰的拿破崙也被子彈削去了
尾巴尖。但人類也為此付出了代價──三個人的頭顱被拳師
的鐵蹄打破；一個人的肚子挨了重重的一下牛犄角；還有一
個人，褲子幾乎被傑西和藍鈴撕毀了。給拿破崙作貼身警衛
的那九條狗，奉命在樹籬的遮掩下繞道而行，在敵人的側翼
突然出現，凶猛地吼叫起來。一見大事不好，弗雷德里克便
招呼他的同夥倉皇地撤了出去。動物們直追到了田野盡頭，
在他們被迫爬上滿布荊棘的藩籬逃生時，最後踹上幾腳。

　　動物們勝利了，但都已是疲憊不堪，鮮血淋漓。他們一
瘸一拐地走回農莊。看到昨日還是親愛的同志今天卻橫屍在
草地上，不禁悲從中來，淚流滿面。他們在那個曾矗立著風
車的地方靜默了好長時間。的的確確，風車沒了，他們辛勤
勞動的成果已不見半點蹤跡，甚至地基也被炸毀了一部分，
而且這麼一來，要想再建風車，情況也非同上一次可比了。
上一次還可以利用剩下的石頭，可這次卻連石頭也沒了──
爆炸把石頭拋到幾百碼以外，好像這兒從來就是一片空地。

　　走近農莊的時候，史奎爾朝他們蹦蹦跳跳地走了過來，
沒有誰記得曾在戰鬥的時候看到過他，而他此時卻心滿意足
得搖頭擺尾。「勝利了！」他喊道。接著，動物們聽見了典
禮的槍聲從農莊裡傳了出來。

「爲什麼要開槍？」拳師不解地問。

「爲什麼？當然是爲了慶祝我們的勝利！」史奎爾嚷道。

「什麼勝利？」拳師問。他的膝蓋還在流血，又丟了一隻蹄鐵，蹄子也綻裂了，另外還有十二顆子彈擊中了他的後腿。

「什麼勝利？同志們，難道我們沒有從我們的領土上──從神聖的動物農莊的領土上趕跑敵人嗎？」

「但他們毀了風車，我們已經爲了風車辛苦了整整兩年！」

「那有什麼？我們會再蓋一座。我們高興的話就建它六座。同志們，你們不瞭解，我們已經幹了一件多麼了不起的事。敵人曾佔領了我們腳下這塊土地。而現在呢，多虧拿破崙同志的領導，我們重新奪回了每一寸的土地！」

「然而我們奪回的只是我們本來就有的，」拳師又說道。

「這就是我們的勝利，」史奎爾不以爲然。

他們一瘸一拐地走進場院。拳師腿皮下的子彈使他疼痛難忍。他知道，擺在他面前的，將是一項從地基開始再建風

車的沉重勞動，他知道應該振作起來。但是，他也第一次想到，自己已十一歲了，身體的狀況已今非昔比。

但當動物們看到那面綠旗在飄揚，聽到再次鳴槍——共響了七下，聽到拿破崙的演說，聽到他對他們的行動的祝賀，他們似乎覺得，歸根究柢，他們的確是取得了巨大的勝利。大家為在戰鬥中罹難的動物們安排了一個隆重的葬禮。拳師和克羅薇拉著靈車，拿破崙親自走在隊伍的前頭。大家整整用了兩天時間舉行各種慶祝活動：有唱歌，有演講，還少不了鳴槍，每一個動物都被授予一顆蘋果，每隻家禽還得到了二盎司穀子，每條狗得到了三塊餅乾。這場戰鬥將被命名為「風車之役」，拿破崙還為此設立了一個新的「綠旗勳章」，並授予了他自己。在這一片歡天喜地之中，那個不幸的鈔票事件也就被忘掉了。

慶祝活動過後幾天，豬偶然在地下室裡發現了一箱威士忌——動物們佔領農莊後盤查農舍時遺漏了它。當天晚上，從莊主院子那邊傳出一陣響亮的歌聲，令大家驚奇的是，中間還夾雜著「英格蘭之獸」的旋律。大約在九點半左右，只見拿破崙戴著一頂瓊斯先生的舊圓頂禮帽，從後門出來，在院子裡飛快地跑了一圈，又閃進門不見了。但在第二天早晨，院子內卻是一片沉寂，看不到一頭豬走動，快到九點鐘時，史奎爾出來了，眼神黯淡，尾巴無力地掉在身後，渾身上下病懨懨的。他把大家叫道一起，傳達了一個沉痛的消

息——拿破崙同志病危！

　　一陣哀號油然而起。莊主院子的門外鋪著草墊，於是，大家踮著蹄尖從那兒走過。他們眼中含著熱淚，相互之間不安地詢問：要是領袖拿破崙離開了，我們可該怎麼辦？農莊裡此刻到處都在風傳，說雪球最終還是成功地設法把毒藥摻到拿破崙的食物中了。十一點，雪球出來發布另一項公告，說是拿破崙同志在彌留之際宣布了一項神聖的法令——飲酒者要處死刑。

　　可是到了傍晚，拿破崙卻顯得有些好轉，次日早上，史奎爾就告訴他們說拿破崙正在順利康復。即日夜晚，拿破崙又重新開始工作了。又過了一天，動物們才知道，他早先讓溫普爾在威靈頓買了一些有關蒸餾及釀酒的小冊子。一周後，拿破崙下令，要把果園那邊的小牧場翻一遍土。那牧場原先是打算為退休動物留作養老用的，現在卻說牧草已經耗盡，需要重新耕種；但不久以後便真相大白了，拿破崙準備在那兒播種大麥。

　　大概就在這時，發生了一件奇怪的事情，幾乎每個動物都百思不得其解。這事發生在一天夜裡十二點鐘左右，當時，院子裡傳來一聲巨大的跌撞聲，大家立刻衝出窩棚去看。那天夜晚月光皎潔，在穀倉一頭寫著「七誡」的牆角下，橫著一架斷為兩截的梯子。在大家短暫的震驚下，史奎

爾平躺在梯子邊上，昏迷不醒。他手邊有一盞馬燈，一把漆刷子，一隻打翻的白漆桶。狗當即就把史奎爾圍了起來，待他剛剛甦醒過來，馬上就護送他回到了莊主院子。大家都想不通這是怎麼回事，只有班傑明呶了呶他那長嘴巴，露出一副了然的神情，似乎看出了一點端倪來，但卻什麼也沒說。

幾天後，穆勒在閱讀七誡時注意到，又有另外一條誡律是被大家記錯的。他們本來以為，第五條誡律是「任何動物不得飲酒」，但有兩個字他們卻都忘記了。實際上，那條誡律應該是：「任何動物不得飲酒過度。」

第 9 章

　　拳師身上的傷口過了很久才好。慶祝活動結束後第二
天，大家就又開始爲風車奔忙了。拳師不肯閒著，強忍著傷
痛，不讓大夥察覺。晚上，他悄悄地告訴克羅薇，他的蹄子
疼得厲害，克羅薇就嚼了些草藥給他敷上。她和班傑明都一
再地勸過拳師：幹活適可而止也就是了，用不著太賣命。但
拳師一句也聽不進去。他說，他實在很希望在能退休之前親
眼看到風車竣工。

　　說到退休，還是有必要回顧一下當初的律法。一開始，
動物農莊的法律規定不同動物的退休年齡分別爲：馬和豬
十二歲，牛十四歲，狗九歲，羊七歲，雞和鵝五歲，而且，
退休以後還會按時領取一份優厚的養老津貼。雖然至今爲止
還沒有一個動物眞正領到過這份津貼，但近來有關這個話題
的討論卻愈來愈多了。果園那邊的小牧場已被留作種植大
麥，就又有小道消息傳出來說養老院的占地改爲了大牧場的
一角據說，每匹馬的養老津貼是每天五磅穀子，到冬天改爲
每天十五磅乾草，節假日裡還發給一根胡蘿蔔或是一個蘋

果。而拳師的十二歲壽辰就在來年的夏末。

　　這段日子裡大家的生活十分艱困。和去年冬天相比，寒冷有增無減，食物卻更少了。除了豬和狗以外，所有動物的口糧再次被縮減。史奎爾解釋說，在定量上過於教條的平等是違背動物主義原則的。不論在什麼情況下，史奎爾都能極其輕鬆地向其他動物證明，無論表面看來如何，事實上他們絕不缺乏糧食。當然，有時會出於暫時考量而稍稍地調整一下供應量（他總是強調「調整」而從來不提「減少」）。但與瓊斯時代相比，現在的進步是驚人的。史奎爾的論據十分有力，他會用他那尖細的嗓音一口氣念完一大串數字。這些數字反映出，和瓊斯時代相比，他們現在有了更多的燕麥、乾草、蘿蔔，工作的時間更短，飲用水的水質更好，大家的平均壽命也延長了，幼崽的存活率提高了，窩棚裡有了更多的草墊，甚至連跳蚤都減少許多。在這樣強大的宣傳攻勢下，大家終於對這一切深信不疑。說實話，在他們的記憶中，瓊斯和他所代表的那過去的一切幾乎已經在記憶裡被時間沖刷得一乾二淨。他們知道，近來的生活的確艱難，常常是饑寒交迫，全部的時間裡除了工作、吃飯、睡覺別無其他。但毫無疑問，如果這確實很糟的話，那過去就一定比這還糟。再說，那時侯他們都是奴隸，而現在卻享有自由。正像史奎爾常說的，這一點使一切都有了天壤之別。

　　吃飯的嘴更多了。這天，四頭母豬差不多同時都下了小

豬，共有三十一頭之多，全都帶著黑白條斑。誰是他們的父親呢？這並不難猜，因為拿破崙是農莊裡唯一的一頭種豬。有消息說，過些時候，等買好了磚頭和木材，就要在院子的花園裡為這些小豬崽蓋一間學堂。目前則是由拿破崙在廚房裡親自為孩子們充任教師。這些小豬平常都在花園裡活動，而且被告誡不許和其他動物的幼崽一起玩耍。大約與此同時，又頒布了一項規定，說是當其他動物在路上遇到豬時，必須馬上讓到路邊；另外，所有的豬，不論地位高低，均享有星期天在尾巴上戴綠絲帶的特權。

這一年總算是無災無難地過去了，但經濟上依然拮据。建學堂用的磚頭、沙子、石灰和完善風車要用的機器都是不小的開銷。莊主院子裡需要的燈油和蠟燭，拿破崙的食用糖（他禁止其他豬吃糖，因為吃糖會使他們發胖）也得花錢去買。再加上數目不少的日雜品，諸如釘子、繩子、煤、鐵絲、鐵塊和狗食餅乾等等，開銷同樣不小。剩下的那些乾草和一部分馬鈴薯已經賣掉，雞蛋的買賣契約便又增加到每周六百個蛋。因此，在這一年中孵出的小雞數量極少，雞群已經不成雞群了。十二月份已經減少了的口糧，二月份又被削減了一次。為了省油，窩棚裡也禁止點燈。只有豬的生活水準並沒有絲毫的下降。事實上，即使有著上述的種種不利情況，他們的體重卻一直有增無減。二月底的一個下午，有一股動物們從來沒有聞到過的令他們垂涎欲滴的香味，從廚

房那一邊的、瓊斯時代一度被廢棄的小釀造房裡飄過了院子。有動物說，這是蒸大麥的味道。他們貪婪地嗅著香氣，心裡都在暗自猜測：這是不是在為他們的晚餐準備熱乎乎的大麥泥？但是，晚飯時並沒有見到熱乎乎的大麥泥。而且在隨後的那個星期天，大家又聽到了一個新的公告，說是從今往後，大麥要成為豬的專用品。大家這才想起，果園那邊的田裡就早就種上大麥了。不久，又傳出了這樣一個消息，說是現在每頭豬每天都可以領用一品脫啤酒，拿破崙的定額則是半加侖，盛裝在上好的瓷器湯碗裡。

但是，不論日子多麼難熬，只要一想到現在活得比從前體面，就足以彌補這一切。現在是歌聲多，演講多，活動多。拿破崙已經指示，每周應該舉行一次叫做「自發遊行」的活動，目的在於慶祝動物農莊的奮鬥成果和繁榮興旺。每到指定時刻，大家便紛紛放下工作，列隊繞著農莊的邊界遊行：豬帶頭，然後是馬、牛、羊，接著是家禽。狗在隊伍兩側，拿破崙的開道黑公雞走在隊伍的最前頭。拳師和克羅薇還總要扯著一面綠旗，旗上畫著蹄子和犄角以及「拿破崙同志萬歲！」的標語。遊行之後，大家朗誦著對拿破崙的贊詩；接著是演講，由史奎爾報告糧食產量增長的最新資料，一逢高潮還要鳴槍慶賀。羊對「自發遊行」活動最為熱衷，如果哪個動物抱怨（一些動物有時趁豬和狗不在場時會發些牢騷）說這是浪費時間，羊就肯定會響亮地反復著「四條腿

是好漢，兩條腿是壞蛋」，頓時就叫得他們啞口無言。但大
體上說，大家對慶祝活動還是相當興致勃勃的。歸根究柢，
他們發現正是在這些活動當中，他們才感到自己真正是當家
做主了，他們所做的一切都是在追求自身的幸福。想到這
些，大家也就心滿意足了。因而，在歌聲中，在遊戲中，在
史奎爾列舉的數字中，在鳴槍聲中，在公雞的啼叫聲中，在
綠旗的飄揚中，他們至少可以在某些時刻忘掉了自己那還是
饑腸轆轆的空肚子。

四月份，動物農莊宣告成立「動物共和國」。這就意味
著要選舉一位總統。可候選人只有一位——拿破崙，他在大
家的一致推舉下就任總統。同一天，又公布了有關雪球和瓊
斯串通勾結的新證據，其中涉及到很多具體事例。從這些事
例中不難看出，雪球不僅詭計多端地破壞過「牛棚之役」，
而且是公開地為瓊斯作幫兇。他在混戰中做為人類一夥的領
袖，還高喊過「人類萬歲！」有些動物仍記得雪球背上帶著
傷，但那實際上是拿破崙親自咬傷的。

仲夏，烏鴉摩西在失蹤數年之後突然返回。他幾乎沒有
什麼變化，照舊不幹活，照舊喋喋不休地講著「糖果山」的
老一套。誰要是願意聽，他就拍打著翅膀飛到一根樹椿上，
滔滔不絕地講起來：「在那裡，同志們，」他一本正經地，
還用大嘴巴指著天空——「在那裡，就在你們看到的那團烏
雲那邊——那兒有座『糖果山』。那個幸福的國度將是我們

可憐的動物們擺脫了塵世勞動之後的最後歸宿！」不只如此，他甚至還聲稱曾在一次高空飛行中到過那裡，並看到了那裡有一望無際的苜蓿地，而無數的亞麻籽餅和方糖就長在低矮的樹籬上。很多動物為此而神往。他們推想，現實生活充滿了飢餓和勞累，那麼，死後的歸宿應該是無限美好的吧？豬對烏鴉摩西的態度相當微妙，他們語帶輕蔑地稱他那些關於「糖果山」的說法全是一派胡言，卻默許了他留在農莊不勞而獲，每天配給他一基爾啤酒。

拳師在蹄子痊癒之後，工作更加拼命了。其實在這一年，所有的動物都像奴隸一般地工作著。農莊裡除了那些日常勞作和第三次重建風車的事之外，還要給小豬蓋學堂——這一工程是在三月份動工的。有時，在食不果腹的情況下作長時間的勞動的確是難以忍受的，但拳師從沒退縮過。從他的幹勁是看不出他的老態的，他只是外貌上有點小小的變化：皮毛沒有以前那麼光亮，粗壯的腰部似乎也有點萎縮。別的動物說：「等春草茂盛時，拳師就會慢慢恢復過來。」但是，春天來了，拳師卻並沒有長胖。有時，當他在通往礦頂的坡上，用盡全身氣力拉著那些巨型圓石頭的時候，支持他的彷彿只有不懈的意志了。這種時候，他總是一聲不吭，但看上去似乎還隱約見到他口中念念有辭：「我會更加努力工作。」克羅薇和班傑明再三警告他要注意身體，但拳師卻絲毫不予理會。他的十二歲壽辰臨近了，但他沒有放在心

上，一心一意想著的只是在領取養老津貼之前把石頭攢夠。

夏天的一個傍晚，農莊裡突然傳出拳師出事的消息。在這之前，他曾獨自外出，往風車那裡拉了一車石頭。果然，消息是真的。幾分鐘後，兩隻鴿子急速飛來，說：「拳師倒下去了！他現在正側躺在風車那裡，站不起來了！」

農莊裡大約有一半動物衝了出去，趕到建風車的小丘上。拳師就躺在那裡。他在車轅中間伸著脖子，連頭也抬不起來，兩眼無神，兩肋的毛被汗水黏得一團一團的，嘴裡流出一股稀稀的鮮血。看到這般情景，克羅薇一下子跪倒在他的身邊。

「拳師！」她喊道，「你怎麼了？」

「我的肺，」拳師聲音微弱，「沒關係，我想沒有我你們也能建成風車，備用的石頭已經足夠了。我充其量也只有一個月可活了。不瞞你說，我一直盼望著退休。眼看著班傑明也老了，說不定他們會讓他也同時退休，和我作個伴。」

「會有人來幫我們的，」克羅薇叫道，「快，誰快去告訴史奎爾這裡出事了！」

大家立刻跑回農莊向史奎爾報告消息，只有克羅薇和班傑明留了下來。班傑明躺在拳師旁邊，不聲不響地用他的長尾巴為拳師驅趕蒼蠅。過了一刻鐘，史奎爾趕到現場，滿臉

關切。他說拿破崙同志已得知此事，對農莊裡這樣一位最忠誠的成員發生的這種不幸感到十分悲傷，而且正在安排把拳師送往威靈頓的醫院治療。聽到這些，大家不免有些不安，因為除了莫莉和雪球之外，其他動物從未離開過農莊，他們不想把一位生病的同志交給人類。然而，史奎爾毫不費力地說服了他們，他說在威靈頓的獸醫院比在農莊裡能更好地治療拳師的病。大約過了半個小時，拳師有些好轉了，他好不容易才站起來，一跛一跛地回到他的馬廄裡，克羅薇和班傑明已經為他鋪好了一張舒適的稻草床。

此後兩天，拳師就待在他的馬廄裡。豬送來了一大瓶粉色的藥，那是他們在藥櫃裡發現的，由克羅薇在飯後給拳師服用，每天兩次。晚上，她躺在他的棚子裡和他聊天，班傑明為他趕蒼蠅。拳師說他對發生的一切並不遺憾。如果能澈底康復，他希望自己還能再活上三年。他盼望能在大牧場的一角平平靜靜地住上一陣子。那樣的話，他就有空閒時間來學習，以增長才智。他說，他打算利用自己的餘生學習字母表上剩下的二十二個字母。

然而，班傑明和克羅薇只有在收工之後才能和拳師在一起。一天中午，來了一輛車拉走了拳師。當時，大家正在一頭豬的監督下忙著在蘿蔔地裡除草，忽然，他們驚訝地看著班傑明從農莊窩棚那邊飛奔而來，一邊還扯著嗓子大叫著。這是他們第一次見到班傑明如此激動，也是第一次看到他沒

命地奔跑。「快，快！」他大聲喊著，「快來呀！他們要拉走拳師！」沒等豬下命令，大家全都放下了手上的工作，趕緊跑回去了。果然，院子裡停著一輛大篷車，由兩匹馬拉著，車邊上寫著字，駕車人的位置上坐著一個男人，臉色陰沉，頭戴一頂低簷圓禮帽。而拳師的棚子真的空了。

大家圍住車，傷感地說：「再見了，拳師！再見！」

「笨蛋！傻瓜！」班傑明喊著，一邊跳，一邊用他的蹄掌敲打著地面：「傻瓜！你們沒看見車子上寫著什麼嗎？」

這下子，大家猶豫了，全都靜了下來。穆勒試圖去拼讀那些字。可班傑明把她推到了一邊，他在一片死寂中念道：

「『威靈頓，艾夫列・西蒙茲，屠馬商兼煮膠商，皮革商兼供應狗食的骨粉商。』你們不明白這是什麼意思嗎？他們要把拳師拉到宰馬場去！」

聽到這些，所有的動物都突然迸發出一陣恐懼的哭嚎。就在這時，坐在車上的那個人揚鞭催馬，馬車在一溜小跑中離開大院。大家跟在後面，拼命地叫喊著。克羅薇硬擠到最前面去。這時，馬車開始加速，克羅薇也越跑越快，「拳師！」她哭喊道，「拳師！拳師！拳師！」此時，拳師好像聽到了外面的喧囂聲，他那張鼻頭上有著白條紋的臉出現在車後的小窗子裡。

「拳師！」克羅薇淒厲地哭喊道，「拳師！出來！快出來！他們要送你去死！」

所有的動物一齊跟著哭喊起來，「出來，拳師，快出來！」但馬車加速離他們愈來愈遠了。誰也不知道拳師到底有沒有聽見克羅薇的那些話。但不一會，他的臉從窗上消失了，接著車內響起一陣巨大的馬蹄踢蹬聲。他是在試圖踢開車子出來。照理說，只要幾下拳師就能把車廂踢個粉碎。可是天啊！時過境遷，他已沒有力氣了；不一會兒，馬蹄的踢蹬聲漸漸變弱，漸漸消失。奮不顧身的動物們便開始懇求拉車的兩匹馬停下來，「朋友，朋友！」他們大聲呼喊，「別把你們的親兄弟拉去送死！」但是那兩匹愚蠢的畜牲，竟然傻得不知道這是怎麼回事，只管豎起耳朵加速奔跑。拳師的臉再也沒有出現在窗子上。有的動物想跑到前面去關上大門，但是太遲了，一瞬間，馬車就已衝出大門，飛快地消失在大路上。就這樣，再也見不到拳師了。

三天之後，拳師被宣告已死在威靈頓的醫院裡。但是，作為一匹馬，他已經得到了無微不至的照顧。這個消息是由史奎爾當眾宣布的，他說，在拳師生前的最後幾小時裡，他一直守候在場。

「那是我見過的最感人的場面！」他說著，抬起蹄子抹去了一滴淚水，「在最後一刻我守在他的床邊。臨終前，他

幾乎衰弱得說不出話來，他湊在我的耳邊，說他唯一遺憾的是沒有看到風車建成。他最後還低聲地嘟囔著：『同志們，前進！以革命的名義前進，動物農莊萬歲！拿破崙同志萬歲！拿破崙永遠正確。』同志們，這些就是他的臨終遺言。」

講到這裡，史奎爾忽然變了臉色。他沉默了一會兒，用他那雙小眼睛疑神疑鬼地掃視了一下全場，才繼續講下去。

他說，據他所知，拳師給拉走後，農莊上流傳著一個愚蠢的、不懷好意的謠言。有的動物注意到，拉走拳師的馬車上有「屠馬商」的標記，就斷定拳師被送到宰馬場了。幾乎難以置信竟有這麼傻的動物！他擺著尾巴左蹦右跳，憤憤地責問：「從這一點來看，你們真的很瞭解敬愛的領袖拿破崙同志嗎？其實，答案十分簡單，那輛車以前曾歸一個屠馬商所有，但獸醫院已買下了它，不過他們還沒有來得及把舊名字塗掉。正是因為這一點，才引起了大家的誤會。」

聽到這裡，大家才大大地鬆了一口氣。接著，史奎爾繼續繪聲繪影地描述著拳師的臨終囑託和他所受到的優厚優待，還有拿破崙為他不惜一切代價購置貴重藥品等等細節。於是，大家打消了最後一絲疑慮，想到他們的同志是在幸福中死去的，悲痛也就消解了。

在接下來的星期天會議上，拿破崙親自到會，為拳師宣

讀了一篇簡短的悼辭。他說,已經不可能把他們痛失的同志的遺體拉回來並安葬在農莊裡了。但他已指示,用莊主院子花園裡的月桂花做一個大花圈,送到拳師的墓前。並且,豬還打算在幾天以後為拳師舉行一場追悼宴會。最後,拿破崙以「我會更加努力工作」和「拿破崙同志永遠正確」這兩句拳師心愛的格言結束了他的演說。他說,每個動物都應該把這兩句格言作為自己的借鑒,並認真地將之貫徹到實際行動中去。

到了宴會的那一天,一輛雜貨商的馬車從威靈頓駛來,在莊主院子地送了一個大木箱。當天晚上,莊主院子裡傳來了一陣鼓噪的歌聲,在此之後,又響起了另外一種聲音,聽上去像是在激烈地爭吵,這吵鬧聲持續到十一點左右,才在一陣打碎了玻璃的巨響中平靜了下來。一直到第二天中午,莊主院子裡不見任何動靜。同時,又流傳著這樣一個小道消息,說豬先前不知從哪裡籌到了一筆錢,給他們自己買了一箱威士忌。

第10章

　　春去秋來，年復一年。在時光的無情流逝中，壽命較短的動物已經一個個地相繼死去。眼下，除了克羅薇、班傑明、烏鴉摩西和幾頭老豬之外，已經沒有一個能記起革命前的那段歲月了。

　　穆勒死了，藍鈴、傑西和小鉗死了，就連瓊斯也死了，死在不知什麼地方的一個酒鬼家裡。雪球更是早被大家忘掉了，「拳師」也成了一個陌生而模糊的名字。克羅薇也老了，身體已胖得有些過份，關節不再柔韌有力，眼角也總是黏滿眼屎。在兩年前她就應該退休了，但實際上，從來沒有一隻動物真正地享受過退休的待遇，撥出大牧場的一角作為養老院的話題也早就擱到了一邊。

　　如今，拿破崙已是一頭完全成熟的雄豬，腦肥體重，足有三百多磅。史奎爾更是胖得連睜眼往外看都覺得費力。只有班傑明好像超脫得置身於歲月之外，除了鼻子和嘴的周圍有點發灰，幾乎就和過去一個樣子。只是，自從拳師死後，

他比以前更見孤僻和沉默了。

現在，農莊裡的牲口要比以前多得多了，儘管早些年裡對增長的預見要比現在樂觀得多。很多動物是在農莊裡土生土長的，還有一些則是來自別的地方。對於前者，革命在他們的腦子裡只不過是一個朦朦朧朧的傳說，而對於後者，那些往日裡的光榮與夢想在他們更是毫不知情。現在的農莊裡，除了克羅薇，另外還有三匹馬。他們都是好同志，都很勤勞，也都很溫順，只可惜智商不高。照現在的樣子看來，他們中間要是有誰能學到字母表上的「B」那就真要謝天謝地了。對於有關革命和有關「動物主義」的事情，他們是聽到什麼就信什麼，一點兒都不過腦子，如果哪件事情是克羅薇講的那就更是這樣了，因為他們已視克羅薇為母親，對她言聽計從。但是，他們究竟是不是真能弄通這些道理，卻是大可懷疑的。

現在的農莊更加欣欣向榮，也更加井然有序。農莊裡甚至增加了兩塊地，是從皮爾金頓先生那裡買來的。風車最終還是建成了，這裡的艱辛自不必言。而且，農莊裡還有了自己的一台脫粒機和乾草運輸機，新的建築也說得上是鱗次櫛比。就連溫普爾也為自己添置了一輛馬車。稍微有些遺憾的，就是風車最終還是沒能用來發電，而是磨穀子用了，這就使磨穀子成為了農莊的支柱產業，著實獲利良多。如今，大家又忙著修建另一座風車了。據說，等這一座風車建成

了，就要裝上發電機來實現當年的夢想。雖然，當年雪球為大家描述的那種舒適、那種帶電燈和冷熱水的窩棚、那種每周三天工作制，如今已不再被談論了。拿破崙早就斥責說，這些想法是與動物主義的精神背道而馳的。他說，真正的幸福就在於工作勤奮和生活儉樸。

不知道為什麼，反正從表面看上去，農莊似乎已經變得富裕了，但動物們自己卻還是窮得掉渣，只有豬和狗確實是走進了新的生活氣象。也許，部分原因是由於豬和狗的家族都比較龐大吧？和大家不同的是，豬狗這一等級的動物，都是用他們自己的方式從事勞動。正像史奎爾總愛掛在嘴上的那樣，農莊的監督和組織要以一種獨特的方式耗費掉驚人的工作量，而這卻是其他動物因為不知情而無法理解的。例如，史奎爾告訴他們說，豬每天要耗費大量的精力，用來處理那些叫做「文件」、「報告」、「會議記錄」和「備忘錄」等等神祕的事宜。這類文件為數眾多，還必須仔細寫在紙上，而一旦填寫完畢，又得把它們在爐子裡燒掉。史奎爾說，為了農莊的幸福，沒有什麼工作是比這更重要的了。但說歸說，迄今為止，無論是豬是狗，都還沒有親自生產過一粒糧食，而他們仍然為數眾多，食欲還總是出奇地旺盛。

至於其他動物，生活還是一如既往。他們普遍都在挨餓，睡的是草墊，喝的是池塘水，幹的是農活，冬天受寒受凍，夏天蚊蠅纏身。有時，會有些上年紀的動物絞盡腦汁，

從那些淡薄的印象中搜索著回憶的線索，試圖判斷比起到底革命以後的那段日子——就是剛趕走瓊斯的那會兒，現在的情況是更好還是更糟？但誰也不記得了，沒有一件事情可以和現在來做參照，除了史奎爾時常公布的一系列沒完沒了的數字以外，他們沒有任何憑據用來比較，而史奎爾的數字總是千篇一律地表明，所有的事物正變得愈來愈好。大家發現這個問題解釋不清，不管怎麼說，他們現在已很少有時間去思索這類事情。唯有老班傑明，他聲稱對自己那漫長一生中的每個細節都記憶猶新，還說他認識到一切事物在過去沒有、在將來也不會有什麼更好或更糟的區別。因此，飢餓、艱難、失望的現實，都是生活中必然要面臨的東西。這就是生活，誰也不能改變。

不過，大家仍然沒有放棄希望。確切地說，他們身為動物農莊的一員，從來沒有失去自己的榮譽和優越感——一會兒也沒有過。他們的農莊依然是整個國家——所有英倫三島中——唯一的一所歸動物自己所有、並由動物自行管理的農莊。他們中間的成員，就連最年輕的，甚至還有那些來自十幾英里以外農莊的新成員，每每想到這一點，自豪感無不油然而生。當他們聽到鳴槍，看到旗杆上綠旗飄揚，豪情壯志就不免湧上心頭，話題一轉，也就時常提起那史詩般的過去，以及驅除瓊斯、刻寫「七誡」、擊退人類來犯者的偉大戰鬥等等。其實，那些舊日的夢想從未被丟棄。想當年梅傑

預言過的「動物共和國」和那個英格蘭的綠色田野上不再被
人類足跡踐踏的夢想，至今依然是他們的信仰所在。他們依
然相信，總有一天，那個時代會到來——也許不是立刻，也
許今生已無望看到，但它終究是要到來的。而且至今，說不
定就連「英格蘭之獸」這支曲子還在被偷偷地到處傳唱著，
反正農莊裡的每個動物都熟悉它，儘管誰也不敢放聲高歌。
也許，他們處境險惡；也許，他們的希望並沒有全部實現，
但他們很清楚，他們和別的動物不一樣。 如果他們還沒有
吃飽，那也不是因爲把食物拿去餵了暴虐的人類；如果他們
工作艱苦，那至少也是在爲自己辛勞。在他們中間，誰也不
用兩條腿走路，誰也不把誰稱做「主人」，所有的動物一律
平等。

初夏的一天，史奎爾把羊叫了出去。他把他們領到農莊
另一頭一塊長滿樺樹苗的地裡。在史奎爾的監督下，羊在那
裡吃了整整一天樹葉子，到了晚上，他告訴羊說，既然天氣
暖和了，他們就待在那兒算了。然後，他獨自返回了莊主院
子。羊就在那裡待了整整一個星期——對大家來說，也就是
失蹤了一個星期。史奎爾每天都要耗費大量時間和他們泡在
一起。他說他正在給羊教唱一首新歌，因此需要清靜。

一天傍晚，羊回來了。當時，大家才剛剛收工，正走在
回家的路上。突然，從大院裡傳來了一聲馬的悲鳴，大家嚇
了一跳，全都停下了腳步：是克羅薇的聲音，她又嘶叫起

來。於是，大家全都奔跑著衝進了大院。這一下，他們全都看到了那讓克羅薇吃驚大叫的情景：

是一頭豬在用後腿走路。

是的，是史奎爾，他的動作還有點笨拙，好像還不大習慣用這種姿勢支撐他那巨大的身體，但平衡感極佳，正在院子裡蹓躂。不一會，從莊主院子裡又走出一長隊豬，都用後腿在行走。他們走得好壞不一，有一兩頭豬還有點不大穩當，看上去好像更適於找一根棍子支撐著。不過，每頭豬大體上還算走得成功。最後，在一陣非常響亮的狗叫聲和黑公雞尖細的啼叫聲中，拿破崙也親自走出來了。他大模大樣地直立著，眼睛朝四下傲慢地瞥了一下，狗警衛活蹦亂跳地簇擁在他的周圍。

他的蹄子裡捏著一根鞭子。

現場陷入一片死寂。驚訝、恐懼的動物們擠在一起，看著那長長一排的豬慢慢地繞著院子雙腿行走。彷彿這世界已經完全顛倒了。接著，當他們從這場震驚中緩過一點勁的時候，有那麼一瞬間，他們顧不上顧慮任何事——顧不上他們對狗的害怕，顧不上他們多少年來養成的，無論發生什麼事也從不抱怨、從不批評的習慣——馬上要大聲抗議了。但就在這時，像是得到信號似的，所有的羊突然爆發出一陣巨大的咩咩聲：

「四條腿是好漢，兩條腿更是好漢！四條腿是好漢，兩條腿更是好漢！四條腿是好漢，兩條腿更是好漢！」

喊叫聲持續了足有五分鐘。等羊安靜下來以後，大家發現已經錯過抗議的機會了，因為豬已列隊走回了莊主院子。

班傑明感覺到有一個鼻子在他肩上磨蹭。回頭一看，是克羅薇。只見她那一雙衰勞的眼睛比以往更加灰暗。她沒說一句話，輕輕地拽他的鬃毛，領著他轉到大穀倉那一頭，那是寫著「七誡」的地方。他們站在那裡注視著有白字的柏油牆。

「我的眼睛不行了，」她終於說話了，「就是年輕時，我也認不得那上面寫的東西。可是今天一看，這面牆怎麼不同以往了。『七誡』還是過去那樣嗎？班傑明？」

只有這一次，班傑明答應破個例，把牆上寫的東西念給她聽，而今那上面已經沒有別的什麼了，只有一條誡律，它是這樣寫的：

所有動物一律平等
但有些動物比其他動物
更平等

從此以後，大家對一切都見怪不怪了。第二天，所有的豬在農莊監督幹活時，蹄子上都捏著一根鞭子，這算不得稀奇；豬給他們自己買了一台無線電收音機，還正在準備安裝一部電話，也算不得稀奇；他們已經訂閱了《約翰·牛報》、《珍聞報》及《每日鏡報》，也算不得稀奇；拿破崙在莊主院子的花園裡散步時，嘴裡叼著一根煙斗，也算不得稀奇。是的，不必再大驚小怪了。哪怕豬把瓊斯先生的衣服從衣櫃裡拿出來穿在自己身上也沒有什麼大不了的。如今，拿破崙已經親自穿上了一件黑外套和一條特製的馬褲，還綁上了皮綁腿，同時，他心愛的母豬也穿上了一件波紋綢裙子，那裙子是瓊斯夫人過去常在星期天穿的。

一周後的下午，一些馬車駛進農莊。一個由鄰近農莊主組成的代表團已接受邀請來此考察觀光。他們參觀了整個農莊，對一切都讚不絕口，尤其是對風車。那時，動物們正在蘿蔔地裡除草，他們都在埋頭苦幹，很少揚起臉，搞不清他們到底是怕豬還是怕人。

那天晚上，從莊主院子裡傳來一陣陣哄笑聲和歌聲。動物們在混雜的聲音中突然被吸引住了，他們感到好奇，動物和人類第一次在平等關係下濟濟一堂，會是怎樣一幅光景呢？於是大家便不約而同地悄悄往莊主院子的花園爬去。

到了門口，他們又停住了，大概是因為害怕，誰也不敢再往前走，最後還是克羅薇帶頭進去了。他們踮著蹄子，走到房子跟前，那些個頭高的動物就從餐廳的窗戶往裡面看。屋子裡面，在那張長桌子周圍，分坐著六個農莊莊主和六頭最有名望的豬，拿破崙坐在桌子上首的東道主席位上。豬在椅子上顯得相當舒適自在。賓主們一直都在津津有味地打著撲克，但在中間停了一會兒，端起酒杯來準備乾杯。有一個很大的罐子在他們中間傳來傳去，在杯子裡添滿了啤酒。他們都沒注意到窗戶外面有很多詫異的面孔正在往裡面窺探。

狐木農莊的皮爾金頓先生舉著杯子站了起來。他說在乾杯之前，有幾句話得先講一下。

他說，他相信，他自己還有在場的各位都感到十分慶

幸，人類和動物農莊之間持續已久的猜疑和誤解終於結束了。曾有這樣一個時期，無論是他自己，還是在座的諸君，都想不到會有今天的情形。當時，可敬的動物農莊的所有者，曾受到他們的人類鄰居的關注，他情願說這關注是出於一定程度上的顧慮而不是滿懷敵意。錯誤與不幸都曾發生過，錯誤的觀念也曾廣爲流行過。一個由豬所有並由豬經營的農莊也曾讓人類覺得有些名不正言不順，而且還確有給鄰近農莊帶來不安的可能。相當多的農莊主沒有做適當的調查就信口開河地推斷，說在動物農莊裡歪風邪氣正在到處蔓延。他們擔心這種狀況會影響到他們自己的動物，甚至影響到他們的雇員。但現在，所有這些懷疑都已煙消雲散了。今天，他和他的朋友們拜訪了動物農莊，用他們自己的眼睛觀察了農莊的每一個角落。他們發現了什麼呢？這裡不僅有最先進的工作方法，而且紀律嚴明，秩序井然，這應該成爲各地農莊的榜樣。他相信，也敢於肯定，動物農莊裡的下層動物，比全郡的任何動物幹的活都多，吃的飯都少。的確，他和他的代表團成員今天看到了這裡的很多特色之處，並準備立即把這些東西在他們自己的農莊中去貫徹實施。

在即將結束發言的時候，他再次重申了動物農莊及其鄰居之間已經建立的和應該建立的友好感情。在豬和人之間不存在、也不應該存在任何意義上的利害衝突。他們的奮鬥目標和遇到的困難是一般無二的。勞工問題不是到哪裡都相同

嗎？講到這裡，皮爾金頓先生好一會兒樂不可支，他竭力抑制住，下巴都憋得發紫了，最後才蹦出了一句：「如果你們有你們的下層動物在和你們作對，」他說，「我們也有我們的下層階級！」這一句畫龍點睛的話引起了一陣哄堂大笑。皮爾金頓先生再次為他在動物農莊看到的飼料供給少、勞動時間長，普遍的樸素生活等諸多良好現象向豬表示了祝賀。

　　他最後請各位站了起來，斟滿酒杯：「先生們，先生們，我敬你們一杯：為動物農莊的繁榮昌盛乾杯！」

　　一片熱烈的喝彩聲和跺腳聲隨即響起，惹得拿破崙心花怒放。他離開座位，繞著桌子走向皮爾金頓先生，和他碰了杯便一口乾了，待喝采聲一靜下來，依然靠後腿站立著的拿破崙舉蹄示意他也有幾句話要講。

　　這番講話就像拿破崙所有的演講一樣，簡明扼要而又一針見血。他說，他也為那個誤解時代的結束而感到高興。曾經有很長一個時期，流傳著各式各樣不懷好意的謠言 —— 他有理由認為，這些謠言是一些居心叵測的仇敵散布的 —— 說在他和他的同僚的觀念中，有一種主張顛覆的、甚至是根本屬於破壞性的東西。他們一直被看作是企圖煽動鄰近農莊的動物造反。但是，事實是最有說服力的。他們唯一的願望，無論是在過去、現在還是將來，都是與他們的鄰居們和平共處，保持正常的貿易關係。他補充說，他有幸掌管的這個農

莊是一家合營企業。他自己手中的那張地契是歸豬共同所有的。

他說道，他相信任何猜疑都已不在，而最近對農莊的一些慣例的修正會進一步增強他的這一信心。長期以來，農莊裡的動物們保留著一個頗為愚蠢的習慣，那就是互相以「同志」相稱。這要取消。還有一個搞不清是怎麼來的怪癖，就是在每個星期天早上，要列隊走過花園裡一個釘在木椿上的雄豬頭蓋骨。這個也要取消。頭蓋骨已經埋了。客人們也許已經看到那面旗杆上飄揚著的那面綠旗，他們或許已經注意到，過去旗面上畫著的白色蹄子和犄角現在已經消失了。從今以後那面旗將是完全的綠色。

他說，對於皮爾金頓先生的精采而友好的演講，他只有一點要作些簡單的補充修正。皮爾金頓先生一直提到「動物農莊」，他當然不知道了，因為就連他拿破崙自己也只是第一次宣告這件事：「動物農莊」這個名字從今作廢，今後，農莊的名字將恢復成「曼諾農莊」。他相信，這個名字才是它真正應該叫的。

「先生們，」他總結道，「我將給你們以同樣的祝辭，但要以不同的形式。請滿上這一杯，先生們，這就是我的祝辭：『為曼諾農莊的繁榮昌盛乾杯！』」

一陣同樣熱烈而真誠的喝采聲轟然響起，酒也一飲而

盡。但當外面的動物們目不轉睛地看著這一情景時,他們似乎看到了有一些怪事正在發生。豬的面孔上似乎有了些變化。克羅薇那一雙昏花的眼睛掃過了一個接一個面孔:他們有的有五個下巴,有的有四個,有的有三個,但是有什麼東西似乎正在融化消失。接著,熱烈的掌聲結束了,他們又拿起撲克牌,繼續剛才中斷的遊戲。外面的動物們這才悄悄地離開了。

但他們還沒有走出二十碼,又突然停住了。莊主院子裡傳出了一陣吵鬧聲。他們跑回去,又一次透過窗子往裡面看。是的,裡面正在大吵大鬧:既有大喊大叫的,也有捶打桌子的;一邊是疑神疑鬼的銳利目光,另一邊卻在咆哮著矢口否認著什麼。動亂的原因好像是因為拿破崙和皮爾金頓先生同時打出了一張黑桃 A。

十二個嗓門一齊在憤怒地狂叫著,他們竟是如此地相似!而今,不必再問豬的面孔上到底發生了什麼變化。窗外的眼睛從豬看到人,又從人看到豬,再從豬看回到人 —— 但他們已分不出究竟誰是豬,誰是人了。

CHAPTER 1

Mr. Jones, of the Manor Farm, had locked the hen-houses for the night, but was too drunk to remember to shut the pop-holes. With the ring of light from his lantern dancing from side to side, he lurched across the yard, kicked off his boots at the back door, drew himself a last glass of beer from the barrel in the scullery, and made his way up to bed, where Mrs. Jones was already snoring.

As soon as the light in the bedroom went out there was a stirring and a fluttering all through the farm buildings. Word had gone round during the day that old Major, the prize Middle White boar, had had a strange dream on the previous night and wished to communicate it to the other animals. It had been agreed that they should all meet in the big barn as soon as Mr. Jones was safely out of the way. Old Major (so he was always called, though the name under which he had been exhibited was Willingdon Beauty) was so highly regarded on the farm that everyone was quite ready to lose an hour's sleep in order to hear what he had to say.

At one end of the big barn, on a sort of raised platform, Major was already ensconced on his bed of straw, under a lantern which hung from a beam. He was twelve years old and had lately grown rather stout, but he was still a majestic-looking pig, with a wise and benevolent appearance in spite of the fact that his tushes had never been cut. Before long the other animals began to arrive and make themselves comfortable after their different fashions. First came the three dogs, Bluebell, Jessie, and Pincher, and then the pigs, who settled down in the straw immediately in front of the platform. The hens perched themselves on the window-sills, the pigeons fluttered up to the rafters, the sheep and cows lay down behind the pigs and began to chew the cud. The two cart-horses, Boxer and Clover, came in together, walking very slowly and setting down their vast hairy hoofs with great care lest there should be some small animal concealed in the straw. Clover was a stout motherly mare approaching middle life, who had never quite got her figure back after her fourth foal. Boxer was an enormous beast, nearly eighteen hands high, and as strong as any two ordinary horses put together. A white stripe down his nose gave him a somewhat stupid appearance, and in fact he was not of first-rate intelligence, but he was universally respected for his steadiness of character and tremendous powers of work. After the horses came Muriel, the white goat, and Benjamin, the donkey. Benjamin was the oldest animal on the farm, and the worst tempered. He seldom talked, and when he did, it was usually to make some cynical remark — for instance, he would say that God had given him a tail to keep the flies off, but that he would sooner have had no tail and no flies. Alone among the animals on the farm he never laughed. If asked why, he would say that he saw nothing to laugh at. Nevertheless, without openly admitting it, he was devoted to Boxer; the two of them usually spent their Sundays together in the small paddock beyond the orchard, grazing side by side and never speaking.

The two horses had just lain down when a brood of ducklings, which had lost their mother, filed into the barn, cheeping feebly and wandering from side to side to find some place where they would not be trodden on. Clover made a sort of wall round them with her great foreleg, and the ducklings nestled down inside it and promptly fell asleep. At the last moment Mollie, the foolish, pretty white mare who drew Mr. Jones's trap, came mincing daintily in, chewing at a lump of sugar. She took a place near the front and began flirting her white mane, hoping to draw attention to the red ribbons it was plaited with. Last of all came the cat, who looked round, as usual, for the warmest place, and finally squeezed herself in between Boxer and Clover; there she purred contentedly throughout Major's speech without listening to a word of what he was saying.

All the animals were now present except Moses, the tame raven, who slept on a perch behind the back door. When Major saw that they had all made themselves comfortable and were waiting attentively, he cleared his throat and began:

"Comrades, you have heard already about the strange dream that I had last night. But I will come to the dream later. I have something else to say first. I do not think, comrades, that I shall be with you for many months longer, and before I die, I feel it my duty to pass on to you such wisdom as I have acquired. I have had a long life, I have

had much time for thought as I lay alone in my stall, and I think I may say that I understand the nature of life on this earth as well as any animal now living. It is about this that I wish to speak to you.

"Now, comrades, what is the nature of this life of ours? Let us face it: our lives are miserable, laborious, and short. We are born, we are given just so much food as will keep the breath in our bodies, and those of us who are capable of it are forced to work to the last atom of our strength; and the very instant that our usefulness has come to an end we are slaughtered with hideous cruelty. No animal in England knows the meaning of happiness or leisure after he is a year old. No animal in England is free. The life of an animal is misery and slavery: that is the plain truth.

"But is this simply part of the order of nature? Is it because this land of ours is so poor that it cannot afford a decent life to those who dwell upon it? No, comrades, a thousand times no! The soil of England is fertile, its climate is good, it is capable of affording food in abundance to an enormously greater number of animals than now inhabit it. This single farm of ours would support a dozen horses, twenty cows, hundreds of sheep — and all of them living in a comfort and a dignity that are now almost beyond our imagining. Why then do we continue in this miserable condition? Because nearly the whole of the produce of our labour is stolen from us by human beings. There, comrades, is the answer to all our problems. It is summed up in a single word — Man.

"Man is the only real enemy we have. Remove Man from the scene, and the root cause of hunger and overwork is abolished for ever.

"Man is the only creature that consumes without producing. He does not give milk, he does not lay eggs, he is too weak to pull the plough, he cannot run fast enough to catch rabbits. Yet he is lord of all the animals. He sets them to work, he gives back to them the bare minimum that will prevent them from starving, and the rest he keeps for himself. Our labour tills the soil, our dung fertilises it, and yet there is not one of us that owns more than his bare skin. You cows that I see before me, how many thousands of gallons of milk have you given during this last year? And what has happened to that milk which should have been breeding up sturdy calves? Every drop of it has gone down the throats of our enemies. And you hens, how many eggs have you laid in this last year, and how many of those eggs ever hatched into chickens? The rest have all gone to market to bring in money for Jones and his men. And you, Clover, where are those four foals you bore, who should have been the support and pleasure of your old age? Each was sold at a year old — you will never see one of them again. In return for your four confinements and all your

labour in the fields, what have you ever had except your bare rations and a stall?

"And even the miserable lives we lead are not allowed to reach their natural span. For myself I do not grumble, for I am one of the lucky ones. I am twelve years old and have had over four hundred children. Such is the natural life of a pig. But no animal escapes the cruel knife in the end. You young porkers who are sitting in front of me, every one of you will scream your lives out at the block within a year. To that horror we all must come — cows, pigs, hens, sheep, everyone. Even the horses and the dogs have no better fate. You, Boxer, the very day that those great muscles of yours lose their power, Jones will sell you to the knacker, who will cut your throat and boil you down for the foxhounds. As for the dogs, when they grow old and toothless, Jones ties a brick round their necks and drowns them in the nearest pond.

"Is it not crystal clear, then, comrades, that all the evils of this life of ours spring from the tyranny of human beings? Only get rid of Man, and the produce of our labour would be our own. Almost overnight we could become rich and free. What then must we do? Why, work night and day, body and soul, for the overthrow of the human race! That is my message to you, comrades: Rebellion! I do not know when that Rebellion will come, it might be in a week or in a hundred years, but I know, as surely as I see this straw beneath my feet, that sooner or later justice will be done. Fix your eyes on that, comrades, throughout the short remainder of your lives! And above all, pass on this message of mine to those who come after you, so that future generations shall carry on the struggle until it is victorious.

"And remember, comrades, your resolution must never falter. No argument must lead you astray. Never listen when they tell you that Man and the animals have a common interest, that the prosperity of the one is the prosperity of the others. It is all lies. Man serves the interests of no creature except himself. And among us animals let there be perfect unity, perfect comradeship in the struggle. All men are enemies. All animals are comrades."

At this moment there was a tremendous uproar. While Major was speaking four large rats had crept out of their holes and were sitting on their hindquarters, listening to him. The dogs had suddenly caught sight of them, and it was only by a swift dash for their holes that the rats saved their lives. Major raised his trotter for silence.

"Comrades," he said, "here is a point that must be settled. The wild creatures, such as rats and rabbits — are they our friends or our enemies? Let us put it to the vote. I propose this question to the meeting: Are rats comrades?"

The vote was taken at once, and it was agreed by an overwhelming majority that rats were comrades. There were only four dissentients, the three dogs and the cat, who was afterwards discovered to have voted on both sides. Major continued:

"I have little more to say. I merely repeat, remember always your duty of enmity towards Man and all his ways. Whatever goes upon two legs is an enemy. Whatever goes upon four legs, or has wings, is a friend. And remember also that in fighting against Man, we must not come to resemble him. Even when you have conquered him, do not adopt his vices. No animal must ever live in a house, or sleep in a bed, or wear clothes, or drink alcohol, or smoke tobacco, or touch money, or engage in trade. All the habits of Man are evil. And, above all, no animal must ever tyrannise over his own kind. Weak or strong, clever or simple, we are all brothers. No animal must ever kill any other animal. All animals are equal.

"And now, comrades, I will tell you about my dream of last night. I cannot describe that dream to you. It was a dream of the earth as it will be when Man has vanished. But it reminded me of something that I had long forgotten. Many years ago, when I was a little pig, my mother and the other sows used to sing an old song of which they knew only the tune and the first three words. I had known that tune in my infancy, but it had long since passed out of my mind. Last night, however, it came back to me in my dream. And what is more, the words of the song also came back-words, I am certain, which were sung by the animals of long ago and have been lost to memory for generations. I will sing you that song now, comrades. I am old and my voice is hoarse, but when I have taught you the tune, you can sing it better for yourselves. It is called Beasts of England."

Old Major cleared his throat and began to sing. As he had said, his voice was hoarse, but he sang well enough, and it was a stirring tune, something between *Clementine* and *La Cucaracha* . The words ran:

Beasts of England, beasts of Ireland,
Beasts of every land and clime,
Hearken to my joyful tidings
Of the golden future time.

Soon or late the day is coming,
Tyrant Man shall be o'erthrown,
And the fruitful fields of England
Shall be trod by beasts alone.

Rings shall vanish from our noses,
And the harness from our back,
Bit and spur shall rust forever,
Cruel whips no more shall crack.

Riches more than mind can picture,
Wheat and barley, oats and hay,
Clover, beans, and mangel-wurzels
Shall be ours upon that day.

Bright will shine the fields of England,
Purer shall its waters be,
Sweeter yet shall blow its breezes
On the day that sets us free.

For that day we all must labour,
Though we die before it break;
Cows and horses, geese and turkeys,
All must toil for freedom's sake.

Beasts of England, beasts of Ireland,
Beasts of every land and clime,
Hearken well and spread my tidings
Of the golden future time.

The singing of this song threw the animals into the wildest excitement. Almost before Major had reached the end, they had begun singing it for themselves. Even the stupidest of them had already picked up the tune and a few of the words, and as for the clever ones, such as the pigs and dogs, they had the entire song by heart within a few minutes. And then, after a few preliminary tries, the whole farm burst out into 'Beasts of England' in tremendous unison. The cows lowed it, the dogs whined it, the sheep bleated it, the horses whinnied it, the ducks quacked it. They were so delighted with the song that they sang it right through five times in succession, and might have continued singing it all night if they had not been interrupted.

Unfortunately, the uproar awoke Mr. Jones, who sprang out of bed, making sure that there was a fox in the yard. He seized the gun which always stood in a corner of his bedroom, and let fly a charge of number 6 shot into the darkness. The pellets buried themselves in the wall of the barn and the meeting broke up hurriedly. Everyone fled to his own sleeping-place. The birds jumped on to their perches, the animals settled down in the straw, and the whole farm was asleep in a moment.

CHAPTER 2

Three nights later old Major died peacefully in his sleep. His body was buried at the foot of the orchard.

This was early in March. During the next three months there was much secret activity. Major's speech had given to the more intelligent animals on the farm a completely new outlook on life. They did not know when the Rebellion predicted by Major would take place, they had no reason for thinking that it would be within their own lifetime, but they saw clearly that it was their duty to prepare for it. The work of teaching and organising the others fell naturally upon the pigs, who were generally recognised as being the cleverest of the animals. Pre-eminent among the pigs were two young boars named Snowball and Napoleon, whom Mr. Jones was breeding up for sale. Napoleon was a large, rather fierce-looking Berkshire boar, the only Berkshire on the farm, not much of a talker, but with a reputation for getting his own way. Snowball was a more vivacious pig than Napoleon, quicker in speech and more inventive, but was not considered to have the same depth of character.

All the other male pigs on the farm were porkers. The best known among them was a small fat pig named Squealer, with very round cheeks, twinkling eyes, nimble movements, and a shrill voice. He was a brilliant talker, and when he was arguing some difficult point he had a way of skipping from side to side and whisking his tail which was somehow very persuasive. The others said of Squealer that he could turn black into white.

These three had elaborated old Major's teachings into a complete system of thought, to which they gave the name of Animalism. Several nights a week, after Mr. Jones was asleep, they held secret meetings in the barn and expounded the principles of Animalism to the others. At the beginning they met with much stupidity and apathy. Some of the animals talked of the duty of loyalty to Mr. Jones, whom they referred to as "Master," or made elementary remarks such as "Mr. Jones feeds us. If he were gone, we should starve to death." Others asked such questions as "Why should we care what happens after we are dead?" or "If this Rebellion is to happen anyway, what difference does it make whether we work for it or not?", and the pigs had great difficulty in making them see that this was contrary to the spirit of Animalism. The stupidest questions of all were asked by Mollie, the white mare. The very first question she asked Snowball was:

"Will there still be sugar after the Rebellion?"

"No," said Snowball firmly. "We have no means of making sugar on this farm. Besides, you do not need sugar. You will have all the oats and hay you want."

"And shall I still be allowed to wear ribbons in my mane?" asked Mollie.

"Comrade," said Snowball, "those ribbons that you are so devoted to are the badge of slavery. Can you not understand that liberty is worth more than ribbons?"

Mollie agreed, but she did not sound very convinced.

The pigs had an even harder struggle to counteract the lies put about by Moses, the tame raven. Moses, who was Mr. Jones's especial pet, was a spy and a tale-bearer, but he was also a clever talker. He claimed to know of the existence of a mysterious country called Sugarcandy Mountain, to which all animals went when they died. It was situated somewhere up in the sky, a little distance beyond the clouds, Moses said. In Sugarcandy Mountain it was Sunday seven days a week, clover was in season all the year round, and lump sugar and linseed cake grew on the hedges. The animals hated Moses because he told tales and did no work, but some of them believed in Sugarcandy Mountain, and the pigs had to argue very hard to persuade them that there was no such place.

Their most faithful disciples were the two cart-horses, Boxer and Clover. These two had great difficulty in thinking anything out for themselves, but having once

accepted the pigs as their teachers, they absorbed everything that they were told, and passed it on to the other animals by simple arguments. They were unfailing in their attendance at the secret meetings in the barn, and led the singing of 'Beasts of England', with which the meetings always ended.

Now, as it turned out, the Rebellion was achieved much earlier and more easily than anyone had expected. In past years Mr. Jones, although a hard master, had been a capable farmer, but of late he had fallen on evil days. He had become much disheartened after losing money in a lawsuit, and had taken to drinking more than was good for him. For whole days at a time he would lounge in his Windsor chair in the kitchen, reading the newspapers, drinking, and occasionally feeding Moses on crusts of bread soaked in beer. His men were idle and dishonest, the fields were full of weeds, the buildings wanted roofing, the hedges were neglected, and the animals were underfed.

June came and the hay was almost ready for cutting. On Midsummer's Eve, which was a Saturday, Mr. Jones went into Willingdon and got so drunk at the Red Lion that he did not come back till midday on Sunday. The men had milked the cows in the early morning and then had gone out rabbiting, without bothering to feed the animals. When Mr. Jones got back he immediately went to sleep on the drawing-room sofa with the News of the World over his face, so that when evening came, the animals were still unfed. At last they could stand it no longer. One of the cows broke in the door of the store-shed with her horn and all the animals began to help themselves from the bins. It was just then that Mr. Jones woke up. The next moment he and his four men were in the store-shed with whips in their hands, lashing out in all directions. This was more than the hungry animals could bear. With one accord, though nothing of the kind had been planned beforehand, they flung themselves upon their tormentors. Jones and his men suddenly found themselves being butted and kicked from all sides. The situation was quite out of their control. They had never seen animals behave like this before, and this sudden uprising of creatures whom they were used to thrashing and maltreating just as they chose, frightened them almost out of their wits. After only a moment or two they gave up trying to defend themselves and took to their heels. A minute later all five of them were in full flight down the cart-track that led to the main road, with the animals pursuing them in triumph.

Mrs. Jones looked out of the bedroom window, saw what was happening, hurriedly flung a few possessions into a carpet bag, and slipped out of the farm by another way. Moses sprang off his perch and flapped after her, croaking loudly. Meanwhile the animals had chased Jones and his men out on to the road and slammed the five-barred gate

behind them.

And so, almost before they knew what was happening, the Rebellion had been successfully carried through: Jones was expelled, and the Manor Farm was theirs.

For the first few minutes the animals could hardly believe in their good fortune. Their first act was to gallop in a body right round the boundaries of the farm, as though to make quite sure that no human being was hiding anywhere upon it; then they raced back to the farm buildings to wipe out the last traces of Jones's hated reign. The harness-room at the end of the stables was broken open; the bits, the nose-rings, the dog-chains, the cruel knives with which Mr. Jones had been used to castrate the pigs and lambs, were all flung down the well. The reins, the halters, the blinkers, the degrading nosebags, were thrown on to the rubbish fire which was burning in the yard. So were the whips. All the animals capered with joy when they saw the whips going up in flames. Snowball also threw on to the fire the ribbons with which the horses' manes and tails had usually been decorated on market days.

"Ribbons," he said, "should be considered as clothes, which are the mark of a human being. All animals should go naked."

When Boxer heard this he fetched the small straw hat which he wore in summer to keep the flies out of his ears, and flung it on to the fire with the rest.

In a very little while the animals had destroyed everything that reminded them of Mr. Jones. Napoleon then led them back to the store-shed and served out a double ration of corn to everybody, with two biscuits for each dog. Then they sang 'Beasts of England' from end to end seven times running, and after that they settled down for the night and slept as they had never slept before.

But they woke at dawn as usual, and suddenly remembering the glorious thing that had happened, they all raced out into the pasture together. A little way down the pasture there was a knoll that commanded a view of most of the farm. The animals rushed to the top of it and gazed round them in the clear morning light. Yes, it was theirs — everything that they could see was theirs! In the ecstasy of that thought they gambolled round and round, they hurled themselves into the air in great leaps of excitement. They rolled in the dew, they cropped mouthfuls of the sweet summer grass, they kicked up clods of the black earth and snuffed its rich scent. Then they made a tour of inspection of the whole farm and surveyed with speechless admiration the ploughland, the hayfield, the orchard, the pool, the spinney. It was as though they had never seen these things before, and even now they could hardly believe that it was all their own.

Then they filed back to the farm buildings and halted in silence outside the door of the farmhouse. That was

theirs too, but they were frightened to go inside. After a moment, however, Snowball and Napoleon butted the door open with their shoulders and the animals entered in single file, walking with the utmost care for fear of disturbing anything. They tiptoed from room to room, afraid to speak above a whisper and gazing with a kind of awe at the unbelievable luxury, at the beds with their feather mattresses, the looking-glasses, the horsehair sofa, the Brussels carpet, the lithograph of Queen Victoria over the drawing-room mantelpiece. They were just coming down the stairs when Mollie was discovered to be missing. Going back, the others found that she had remained behind in the best bedroom. She had taken a piece of blue ribbon from Mrs. Jones's dressing-table, and was holding it against her shoulder and admiring herself in the glass in a very foolish manner. The others reproached her sharply, and they went outside. Some hams hanging in the kitchen were taken out for burial, and the barrel of beer in the scullery was stove in with a kick from Boxer's hoof, otherwise nothing in the house was touched. A unanimous resolution was passed on the spot that the farmhouse should be preserved as a museum. All were agreed that no animal must ever live there.

The animals had their breakfast, and then Snowball and Napoleon called them together again.

"Comrades," said Snowball, "it is half-past six and

we have a long day before us. Today we begin the hay harvest. But there is another matter that must be attended to first."

The pigs now revealed that during the past three months they had taught themselves to read and write from an old spelling book which had belonged to Mr. Jones's children and which had been thrown on the rubbish heap. Napoleon sent for pots of black and white paint and led the way down to the five-barred gate that gave on to the main road. Then Snowball (for it was Snowball who was best at writing) took a brush between the two knuckles of his trotter, painted out MANOR FARM from the top bar of the gate and in its place painted ANIMAL FARM. This was to be the name of the farm from now onwards. After this they went back to the farm buildings, where Snowball and Napoleon sent for a ladder which they caused to be set against the end wall of the big barn. They explained that by their studies of the past three months the pigs had succeeded in reducing the principles of Animalism to Seven Commandments. These Seven Commandments would now be inscribed on the wall; they would form an unalterable law by which all the animals on Animal Farm must live for ever after. With some difficulty (for it is not easy for a pig to balance himself on a ladder) Snowball climbed up and set to work, with Squealer a few rungs below him holding the paint-pot. The Commandments

were written on the tarred wall in great white letters that could be read thirty yards away. They ran thus:

THE SEVEN COMMANDMENTS

1. Whatever goes upon two legs is an enemy.
2. Whatever goes upon four legs, or has wings, is a friend.
3. No animal shall wear clothes.
4. No animal shall sleep in a bed.
5. No animal shall drink alcohol.
6. No animal shall kill any other animal.
7. All animals are equal.

It was very neatly written, and except that "friend" was written "freind" and one of the "S's" was the wrong way round, the spelling was correct all the way through. Snowball read it aloud for the benefit of the others. All the animals nodded in complete

THE SEVEN COMMANDMENTS

1. Whatever goes upon two legs is enemy.

2. Whatever goes upon four legs, or has wings, is a friend.

3. No

agreement, and the cleverer ones at once began to learn the Commandments by heart.

"Now, comrades," cried Snowball, throwing down the paint-brush, "to the hayfield! Let us make it a point of honour to get in the harvest more quickly than Jones and his men could do."

But at this moment the three cows, who had seemed uneasy for some time past, set up a loud lowing. They had not been milked for twenty-four hours, and their udders were almost bursting. After a little thought, the pigs sent for buckets and milked the cows fairly successfully, their trotters being well adapted to this task. Soon there were five buckets of frothing creamy milk at which many of the animals looked with considerable

interest.

"What is going to happen to all that milk?" said someone.

"Jones used sometimes to mix some of it in our mash," said one of the hens.

"Never mind the milk, comrades!" cried Napoleon, placing himself in front of the buckets. "That will be attended to. The harvest is more important. Comrade Snowball will lead the way. I shall follow in a few minutes. Forward, comrades! The hay is waiting."

So the animals trooped down to the hayfield to begin the harvest, and when they came back in the evening it was noticed that the milk had disappeared.

CHAPTER 3

How they toiled and sweated to get the hay in! But their efforts were rewarded, for the harvest was an even bigger success than they had hoped.

Sometimes the work was hard; the implements had been designed for human beings and not for animals, and it was a great drawback that no animal was able to use any tool that involved standing on his hind legs. But the pigs were so clever that they could think of a way round every difficulty. As for the horses, they knew every inch of the field, and in fact understood the business of mowing and raking far better than Jones and his men had ever done. The pigs did not actually work, but directed and supervised the others. With their superior knowledge it was natural that they should assume the leadership. Boxer and Clover would harness themselves to the cutter or the horse-rake (no bits or reins were needed in these days, of course) and tramp steadily round and round the field with a pig walking behind and calling out "Gee up, comrade!" or "Whoa back, comrade!" as the case might be. And every animal

Animal Farm

down to the
humblest
worked at
turning the hay
and gathering it.
Even the ducks
and hens toiled to
and fro all day in the
sun, carrying tiny wisps of
hay in their beaks. In the end
they finished the harvest in two
days' less time than it had usually
taken Jones and his men. Moreover, it was
the biggest harvest that the farm had ever
seen. There was no wastage whatever;
the hens and ducks with their
sharp eyes had gathered up the
very last stalk. And not an
animal on the farm had stolen
so much as a mouthful.

All through that summer
the work of the farm went
like clockwork. The animals
were happy as they had never
conceived it possible to be.
Every mouthful of food was an

acute positive pleasure, now that it was truly their own food, produced by themselves and for themselves, not doled out to them by a grudging master. With the worthless parasitical human beings gone, there was more for everyone to eat. There was more leisure too, inexperienced though the animals were. They met with many difficulties — for instance, later in the year, when they harvested the corn, they had to tread it out in the ancient style and blow away the chaff with their breath, since the farm possessed no threshing machine — but the pigs with their cleverness and Boxer with his tremendous muscles always pulled them through. Boxer was the admiration of everybody. He had been a hard worker even in Jones's time, but now he seemed more like three horses than one; there were days when the entire work of the farm seemed to rest on his mighty shoulders. From morning to night he was pushing and pulling, always at the spot where the work was hardest. He had made an arrangement with one of the cockerels to call him in the mornings half an hour earlier than anyone else, and would put in some volunteer labour at whatever seemed to be most needed, before the regular day's work began. His answer to every problem, every setback, was "I will work harder!" — which he had adopted as his personal motto.

But everyone worked according to his capacity. The hens and ducks, for instance, saved five bushels of corn at the harvest by gathering up the stray grains. Nobody stole,

nobody grumbled over his rations, the quarrelling and biting and jealousy which had been normal features of life in the old days had almost disappeared. Nobody shirked — or almost nobody. Mollie, it was true, was not good at getting up in the mornings, and had a way of leaving work early on the ground that there was a stone in her hoof. And the behaviour of the cat was somewhat peculiar. It was soon noticed that when there was work to be done the cat could never be found. She would vanish for hours on end, and then reappear at meal-times, or in the evening after work was over, as though nothing had happened. But she always made such excellent excuses, and purred so affectionately, that it was impossible not to believe in her good intentions. Old Benjamin, the donkey, seemed quite unchanged since the Rebellion. He did his work in the same slow obstinate way as he had done it in Jones's time, never shirking and never volunteering for extra work either. About the Rebellion and its results he would express no opinion. When asked whether he was not happier now that Jones was gone, he would say only "Donkeys live a long time. None of you has ever seen a dead donkey," and the others had to be content with this cryptic answer.

On Sundays there was no work. Breakfast was an hour later than usual, and after breakfast there was a ceremony which was observed every week without fail. First came the hoisting of the flag. Snowball had found in the harness-

room an old green tablecloth of
Mrs. Jones's and had painted on it
a hoof and a horn in white. This
was run up the flagstaff in the
farmhouse garden every Sunday
morning. The flag was green,
Snowball explained, to represent the green fields of
England, while the hoof and horn signified the
future Republic of the Animals which would arise
when the human race had been finally overthrown.
After the hoisting of the flag all the animals trooped into
the big barn for a general assembly which was known as
the Meeting. Here the work of the coming week was
planned out and resolutions were put forward and debated.
It was always the pigs who put forward the resolutions. The
other animals understood how to vote, but could never
think of any resolutions of their own. Snowball and
Napoleon were by far the most active in the debates. But it
was noticed that these two were never in agreement:
whatever suggestion either of them made, the other could
be counted on to oppose it. Even when it was resolved —
a thing no one could object to in itself — to set aside the
small paddock behind the orchard as a home of rest for
animals who were past work, there was a stormy debate
over the correct retiring age for each class of animal. The
Meeting always ended with the singing of 'Beasts of

England' , and the afternoon was given up to recreation.

The pigs had set aside the harness-room as a headquarters for themselves. Here, in the evenings, they studied blacksmithing, carpentering, and other necessary arts from books which they had brought out of the farmhouse. Snowball also busied himself with organising the other animals into what he called Animal Committees. He was indefatigable at this. He formed the Egg Production Committee for the hens, the Clean Tails League for the cows, the Wild Comrades' Re-education Committee (the object of this was to tame the rats and rabbits), the Whiter Wool Movement for the sheep, and various others, besides instituting classes in reading and writing. On the whole, these projects were a failure. The attempt to tame the wild creatures, for instance, broke down almost immediately. They continued to behave very much as before, and when treated with generosity, simply took advantage of it. The cat joined the Re-education Committee and was very active in it for some days. She was seen one day sitting on a roof and talking to some sparrows who were just out of her reach. She was telling them that all animals were now comrades and that any sparrow who chose could come and perch on her paw; but the sparrows kept their distance.

The reading and writing classes, however, were a great success. By the autumn almost every animal on the farm was literate in some degree.

As for the pigs, they could already read and write perfectly. The dogs learned to read fairly well, but were not interested in reading anything except the Seven Commandments. Muriel, the goat, could read somewhat better than the dogs, and sometimes used to read to the others in the evenings from scraps of newspaper which she found on the rubbish heap. Benjamin could read as well as any pig, but never exercised his faculty. So far as he knew, he said, there was nothing worth reading. Clover learnt the whole alphabet, but could not put words together. Boxer could not get beyond the letter D. He would trace out A, B, C, D, in the dust with his great hoof, and then would stand staring at the letters with his ears back, sometimes shaking his forelock, trying with all his might to remember what came next and never succeeding. On several occasions, indeed, he did learn E, F, G, H, but by the time he knew them, it was always discovered that he had forgotten A, B, C, and D. Finally he decided to be content with the first four letters, and used to write them out once or twice every day to refresh his memory. Mollie refused to learn any but the six letters which spelt her own name. She would form these very neatly out of pieces of twig, and would then decorate them with a flower or two and walk round them admiring them.

None of the other animals on the farm could get

further than the letter A. It was also found that the stupider animals, such as the sheep, hens, and ducks, were unable to learn the Seven Commandments by heart. After much thought Snowball declared that the Seven Commandments could in effect be reduced to a single maxim, namely:

"Four legs good, two legs bad." This, he said, contained the essential principle of Animalism.

Whoever had thoroughly grasped it would be safe from human influences. The birds at first objected, since it seemed to them that they also had two legs, but Snowball proved to them that this was not so.

"A bird's wing, comrades," he said, "is an organ of propulsion and not of manipulation. It should therefore be regarded as a leg. The distinguishing mark of man is the HAND, the instrument with which he does all his mischief."

The birds did not understand Snowball's long words, but they accepted his explanation, and all the humbler animals set to work to learn the new maxim by heart. FOUR LEGS GOOD, TWO LEGS BAD, was inscribed on the end wall of the barn, above the Seven Commandments and in bigger letters. When they had once got it by heart, the sheep developed a great liking for this maxim, and often as they lay in the field they would all start bleating "Four legs good, two legs bad! Four legs good, two legs bad!" and keep it up for hours on end, never

growing tired of it.

Napoleon took no interest in Snowball's committees. He said that the education of the young was more important than anything that could be done for those who were already grown up. It happened that Jessie and Bluebell had both whelped soon after the hay harvest, giving birth between them to nine sturdy puppies. As soon as they were weaned, Napoleon took them away from their mothers, saying that he would make himself responsible for their education. He took them up into a loft which could only be reached by a ladder from the harness-room, and there kept them in such seclusion that the rest of the farm soon forgot their existence.

The mystery of where the milk went to was soon cleared up. It was mixed every day into the pigs' mash.

The early apples were now ripening, and the grass of the orchard was littered with windfalls. The animals had assumed as a matter of course that these would be shared out equally; one day, however, the order went forth that all the windfalls were to be collected and brought to the harness-room for the use of the pigs. At this some of the other animals murmured, but it was no use. All the pigs were in full agreement on this point, even Snowball and Napoleon. Squealer was sent to make the necessary explanations to the others.

"Comrades!" he cried. "You do not imagine, I

hope, that we pigs are doing this in a spirit of selfishness and privilege? Many of us actually dislike milk and apples. I dislike them myself. Our sole object in taking these things is to preserve our health. Milk and apples (this has been proved by Science, comrades) contain substances absolutely necessary to the well-being of a pig. We pigs are brainworkers. The whole management and organisation of this farm depend on us. Day and night we are watching over your welfare. It is for YOUR sake that we drink that milk and eat those apples. Do you know what would happen if we pigs failed in our duty? Jones would come back! Yes, Jones would come back! Surely, comrades," cried Squealer almost pleadingly, skipping from side to side and whisking his tail, "surely there is no one among you who wants to see Jones come back?"

Now if there was one thing that the animals were completely certain of, it was that they did not want Jones back. When it was put to them in this light, they had no more to say. The importance of keeping the pigs in good health was all too obvious. So it was agreed without further argument that the milk and the windfall apples (and also the main crop of apples when they ripened) should be reserved for the pigs alone.

CHAPTER 4

By the late summer the news of what had happened on Animal Farm had spread across half the county. Every day Snowball and Napoleon sent out flights of pigeons whose instructions were to mingle with the animals on neighbouring farms, tell them the story of the Rebellion, and teach them the tune of 'Beasts of England'.

Most of this time Mr. Jones had spent sitting in the taproom of the Red Lion at Willingdon, complaining to anyone who would listen of the monstrous injustice he had suffered in being turned out of his property by a pack of good-for-nothing animals. The other farmers sympathised in principle, but they did not at first give him much help. At heart, each of them was secretly wondering whether he could not somehow turn Jones's misfortune to his own advantage. It was lucky that the owners of the two farms which adjoined Animal Farm were on permanently bad terms. One of them, which was named Foxwood, was a large, neglected, old-fashioned farm, much overgrown by woodland, with all its pastures worn out and its hedges in a disgraceful condition. Its owner, Mr. Pilkington, was an easy-going gentleman farmer who spent most of his time in fishing or hunting according to the season. The other farm, which was called Pinchfield, was smaller and better kept. Its owner was a Mr. Frederick, a tough, shrewd man, perpetually involved in lawsuits and with a name for driving hard bargains. These two disliked each other so much that it was difficult for them to come to any agreement, even in defence of their own interests.

Nevertheless, they were both thoroughly frightened by the rebellion on Animal Farm, and very anxious to prevent their own animals from learning too much about it. At first they pretended to laugh to scorn the idea of animals managing a farm for themselves. The whole thing would be over in a fortnight, they said. They put it about that the animals on the Manor Farm (they insisted on calling it the Manor Farm; they would not tolerate the name "Animal Farm") were perpetually fighting among themselves and were also rapidly starving to death. When time passed and the animals had evidently not starved to death, Frederick and Pilkington changed their tune and began to talk of the terrible wickedness that now flourished on Animal Farm. It was given out that the animals there practised cannibalism, tortured one another with red-hot horseshoes, and had their females in common. This was what came of rebelling against the laws of Nature, Frederick and Pilkington said.

However, these stories were never fully believed. Rumours of a wonderful farm, where the human beings had been turned out and the animals managed their own affairs, continued to circulate in vague and distorted forms, and throughout that year a wave of rebelliousness ran through the countryside. Bulls which had always been tractable suddenly turned savage, sheep broke down hedges and devoured the clover, cows kicked the pail over, hunters refused their fences and shot their riders on to the other side. Above all, the tune and even the words of 'Beasts of England' were known everywhere. It had spread with astonishing speed. The human beings could not contain their rage when they heard this song, though they pretended to think it merely ridiculous. They could not understand, they said, how even animals could bring themselves to sing such contemptible rubbish. Any animal caught singing it was given a flogging on the spot. And yet the song was irrepressible. The blackbirds whistled it in the hedges, the pigeons cooed it in the elms, it got into the din of the smithies and the tune of the church bells. And when the human beings listened to it, they secretly trembled, hearing in it a prophecy of their future doom.

Early in October, when the corn was cut and stacked and some of it was already threshed, a flight of pigeons came whirling through the air and alighted in the yard of Animal Farm in the wildest excitement. Jones and all his men, with half a dozen others from Foxwood and Pinchfield, had entered the five-barred gate and were coming up the cart-track that led to the farm. They were all carrying sticks, except Jones, who was marching ahead with a gun in his hands. Obviously they were going to attempt the recapture of the farm.

This had long been expected, and all preparations had been made. Snowball, who had studied an old book of Julius Caesar's campaigns which he had found in the farmhouse, was in charge of the defensive operations. He gave his orders quickly, and in a couple of minutes every animal was at his post.

As the human beings approached the farm buildings, Snowball launched his first attack. All the pigeons, to the number of thirty-five, flew to and fro over the men's heads and muted upon them from mid-air; and while the men were dealing with this, the geese, who had been hiding behind the hedge, rushed out and pecked viciously at the calves of their legs.

However, this was only a light skirmishing manoeuvre, intended to create a little disorder, and the men easily drove the geese off with their sticks. Snowball now launched his second line of attack. Muriel, Benjamin, and all the sheep, with Snowball at the head of them, rushed forward and prodded and butted the men from every side, while Benjamin turned around and lashed at them with his small hoofs. But once again the men, with their sticks and their hobnailed boots, were too strong for them; and suddenly, at a squeal from Snowball, which was the signal for retreat, all the animals turned and fled through the gateway into the yard.

The men gave a shout of triumph. They saw, as they imagined, their enemies in flight, and they rushed after them in disorder. This was just what Snowball had intended. As soon as they were well inside the yard, the three horses, the three cows, and the rest of the pigs, who had been lying in ambush in the cowshed, suddenly emerged in their rear, cutting them off. Snowball now gave the signal for the charge. He himself dashed straight for Jones. Jones saw him coming, raised his gun and fired. The pellets scored bloody streaks along Snowball's back, and a sheep dropped dead. Without halting for an instant, Snowball flung his fifteen stone against Jones's legs. Jones was hurled into a pile of dung and his gun flew out of his hands.

But the most terrifying spectacle of all was Boxer, rearing up on his hind legs and striking out with his great iron-shod hoofs like a stallion. His very first blow took a stable-lad from Foxwood on the skull and stretched him lifeless in the mud. At the sight, several men dropped their sticks and tried to run. Panic overtook them, and the next moment all the animals together were chasing them round

and round the yard. They were gored, kicked, bitten, trampled on. There was not an animal on the farm that did not take vengeance on them after his own fashion. Even the cat suddenly leapt off a roof onto a cowman's shoulders and sank her claws in his neck, at which he yelled horribly. At a moment when the opening was clear, the men were glad enough to rush out of the yard and make a bolt for the main road. And so within five minutes of their invasion they were in ignominious retreat by the same way as they had come, with a flock of geese hissing after them and pecking at their calves all the way.

All the men were gone except one. Back in the yard Boxer was pawing with his hoof at the stable-lad who lay face down in the mud, trying to turn him over. The boy did not stir.

"He is dead," said Boxer sorrowfully. "I had no intention of doing that. I forgot that I was wearing iron shoes. Who will believe that I did not do this on purpose?"

"No sentimentality, comrade!" cried Snowball from whose wounds the blood was still dripping. "War is war. The only good human being is a dead one."

"I have no wish to take life, not even human life," repeated Boxer, and his eyes were full of tears.

"Where is Mollie?" exclaimed somebody.

Mollie in fact was missing. For a moment there was

great alarm; it was feared that the men might have harmed her in some way, or even carried her off with them. In the end, however, she was found hiding in her stall with her head buried among the hay in the manger. She had taken to flight as soon as the gun went off. And when the others came back from looking for her, it was to find that the stable-lad, who in fact was only stunned, had already recovered and made off.

The animals had now reassembled in the wildest excitement, each recounting his own exploits in the battle at the top of his voice. An impromptu celebration of the victory was held immediately. The flag was run up and 'Beasts of England' was sung a number of times, then the sheep who had been killed was given a solemn funeral, a hawthorn bush being planted on her grave. At the graveside Snowball made a little speech, emphasising the need for all animals to be ready to die for Animal Farm if need be.

The animals decided unanimously to create a military decoration, "Animal Hero, First Class," which was conferred there and then on Snowball and Boxer. It consisted of a brass medal (they were really some old horse-brasses which had been found in the harness-room), to be worn on Sundays and holidays. There was also "Animal Hero, Second Class," which was conferred posthumously on the dead sheep.

There was much discussion as to what the battle
should be called. In the end, it was named the Battle of the
Cowshed, since that was where the ambush had been
sprung. Mr. Jones's gun had been found lying in the mud,
and it was known that there was a supply of cartridges in
the farmhouse. It was decided to set the gun up at the foot
of the Flagstaff, like a piece of artillery, and to fire it twice
a year — once on October the twelfth, the anniversary of
the Battle of the Cowshed, and once on Midsummer Day,
the anniversary of the Rebellion.

CHAPTER 5

As winter drew on, Mollie became more and more troublesome. She was late for work every morning and excused herself by saying that she had overslept, and she complained of mysterious pains, although her appetite was excellent. On every kind of pretext she would run away from work and go to the drinking pool, where she would stand foolishly gazing at her own reflection in the water. But there were also rumours of something more serious.

One day, as Mollie strolled blithely into the yard, flirting her long tail and chewing at a stalk of hay, Clover took her aside.

"Mollie," she said, "I have something very serious to say to you. This morning I saw you looking over the hedge that divides Animal Farm from Foxwood. One of Mr. Pilkington's men was standing on the other side of the hedge. And — I was a long way away, but I am almost certain I saw this — he was talking to you and you were allowing him to stroke your nose. What does that mean, Mollie?"

"He didn't! I wasn't! It isn't true!" cried Mollie, beginning to prance about and paw the ground.

"Mollie! Look me in the face. Do you give me your word of honour that that man was not stroking your nose?"

"It isn't true!" repeated Mollie, but she could not look Clover in the face, and the next moment she took to her heels and galloped away into the field.

A thought struck Clover. Without saying anything to the others, she went to Mollie's stall and turned over the straw with her hoof. Hidden under the straw was a little pile of lump sugar and several bunches of ribbon of different colours.

Three days later Mollie disappeared. For some weeks nothing was known of her whereabouts, then the pigeons reported that they had seen her on the other side of Willingdon. She was between the shafts of a smart dogcart painted red and black, which was standing outside a public-house. A fat red-faced man in check breeches and gaiters, who looked like a publican, was stroking her nose and feeding her with sugar. Her coat was newly clipped and she wore a scarlet ribbon round her forelock. She appeared to be enjoying herself, so the pigeons said. None of the animals ever mentioned Mollie again.

In January there came bitterly hard weather. The earth was like iron, and nothing could be done in the fields. Many

meetings were held in the big barn, and the pigs occupied themselves with planning out the work of the coming season. It had come to be accepted that the pigs, who were manifestly cleverer than the other animals, should decide all questions of farm policy, though their decisions had to be ratified by a majority vote. This arrangement would have worked well enough if it had not been for the disputes between Snowball and Napoleon. These two disagreed at every point where disagreement was possible. If one of them suggested sowing a bigger acreage with barley, the other was certain to demand a bigger acreage of oats, and if one of them said that such and such a field was just right for cabbages, the other would declare that it was useless for anything except roots. Each had his own following, and there were some violent debates. At the Meetings Snowball often won over the majority by his brilliant speeches, but Napoleon was better at canvassing support for himself in between times. He was especially successful with the sheep. Of late the sheep had taken to bleating "Four legs good, two legs bad" both in and out of season, and they often interrupted the Meeting with this. It was noticed that they were especially liable to break into "Four legs good, two legs bad" at crucial moments in Snowball's speeches. Snowball had made a close study of some back numbers of the 'Farmer and Stockbreeder' which he had found in the farmhouse, and was full of plans for innovations and

improvements. He talked learnedly about field drains, silage, and basic slag, and had worked out a complicated scheme for all the animals to drop their dung directly in the fields, at a different spot every day, to save the labour of cartage.

Napoleon produced no schemes of his own, but said quietly that Snowball's would come to nothing, and seemed to be biding his time. But of all their controversies, none was so bitter as the one that took place over the windmill.

In the long pasture, not far from the farm buildings, there was a small knoll which was the highest point on the farm. After surveying the ground, Snowball declared that this was just the place for a windmill, which could be made to operate a dynamo and supply the farm with electrical power. This would light the stalls and warm them in winter, and would also run a circular saw, a chaff-cutter, a mangel-slicer, and an electric milking machine. The animals had never heard of anything of this kind before (for the farm was an old-fashioned one and had only the most primitive machinery), and they listened in astonishment while Snowball conjured up pictures of fantastic machines which would do their work for them while they grazed at their ease in the fields or improved their minds with reading and conversation.

Within a few weeks Snowball's plans for the windmill were fully worked out. The mechanical details came mostly

from three books which had belonged to Mr. Jones —
'One Thousand Useful Things to Do About the House', 'Every Man His Own Bricklayer', and 'Electricity for Beginners'.

Snowball used as his study a shed which had once been used for incubators and had a smooth wooden floor, suitable for drawing on. He was closeted there for hours at a time. With his books held open by a stone, and with a piece of chalk gripped between the knuckles of his trotter, he would move rapidly to and fro, drawing in line after line and uttering little whimpers of excitement. Gradually the plans grew into a complicated mass of cranks and cog-wheels, covering more than half the floor, which the other animals found completely unintelligible but very impressive. All of them came to look at Snowball's drawings at least once a day. Even the hens and ducks came, and were at pains not to tread on the chalk marks.

Only Napoleon held aloof. He had declared himself against the windmill from the start. One day, however, he arrived unexpectedly to examine the plans. He walked heavily round the shed, looked closely at every detail of the plans and snuffed at them once or twice, then stood for a little while contemplating them out of the corner of his eye; then suddenly he lifted his leg, urinated over the plans, and walked out without uttering a word.

The whole farm was deeply divided on the subject of

the windmill. Snowball did not deny that to build it would be a difficult business. Stone would have to be carried and built up into walls, then the sails would have to be made and after that there would be need for dynamos and cables. (How these were to be procured, Snowball did not say.) But he maintained that it could all be done in a year. And thereafter, he declared, so much labour would be saved that the animals would only need to work three days a week. Napoleon, on the other hand, argued that the great need of the moment was to increase food production, and that if they wasted time on the windmill they would all starve to death. The animals formed themselves into two factions under the slogan, "Vote for Snowball and the three-day week" and "Vote for Napoleon and the full manger." Benjamin was the only animal who did not side with either faction. He refused to believe either that food would become more plentiful or that the windmill would save work. Windmill or no windmill, he said, life would go on as it had always gone on — that is, badly.

Apart from the disputes over the windmill, there was the question of the defence of the farm. It was fully realised that though the human beings had been defeated in the Battle of the Cowshed they might make another and more determined attempt to recapture the farm and reinstate Mr. Jones. They had all the more reason for doing so because the news of their defeat had spread across the

countryside and made the animals on the neighbouring farms more restive than ever. As usual, Snowball and Napoleon were in disagreement. According to Napoleon, what the animals must do was to procure firearms and train themselves in the use of them. According to Snowball, they must send out more and more pigeons and stir up rebellion among the animals on the other farms. The one argued that if they could not defend themselves they were bound to be conquered, the other argued that if rebellions happened everywhere they would have no need to defend themselves. The animals listened first to Napoleon, then to Snowball, and could not make up their minds which was right; indeed, they always found themselves in agreement with the one who was speaking at the moment.

At last the day came when Snowball's plans were completed. At the Meeting on the following Sunday the question of whether or not to begin work on the windmill was to be put to the vote. When the animals had assembled in the big barn, Snowball stood up and, though occasionally interrupted by bleating from the sheep, set forth his reasons for advocating the building of the windmill. Then Napoleon stood up to reply. He said very quietly that the windmill was nonsense and that he advised nobody to vote for it, and promptly sat down again; he had spoken for barely thirty seconds, and seemed almost indifferent as to the effect he produced. At this Snowball sprang to his feet, and shouting down the sheep, who had begun bleating again, broke into a passionate appeal in favour of the windmill. Until now the animals had been about equally divided in their sympathies, but in a moment Snowball's eloquence had carried them away. In glowing sentences he painted a picture of Animal Farm as it might be when sordid labour was lifted from the animals' backs. His imagination had now run far beyond chaff-cutters and turnip-slicers. Electricity, he said, could operate threshing machines, ploughs, harrows, rollers, and reapers and binders, besides supplying every stall with its own electric light, hot and cold water, and an electric heater. By the time he had finished speaking, there was no doubt as to which way the vote would go. But just at this moment Napoleon stood up and, casting a peculiar sidelong look at Snowball, uttered a high-pitched whimper of a kind no one had ever heard him utter before.

At this there was a terrible baying sound outside, and nine enormous dogs wearing brass-studded collars came bounding into the barn. They dashed straight for Snowball, who only sprang from his place just in time to escape their snapping jaws. In a moment he was out of the door and they were after him. Too amazed and frightened to speak, all the animals crowded through the door to watch the chase. Snowball was racing across the long pasture that led to the road. He was running as only a pig can run, but the

dogs were close on his heels. Suddenly he slipped and it seemed certain that they had him. Then he was up again, running faster than ever, then the dogs were gaining on him again. One of them all but closed his jaws on Snowball's tail, but Snowball whisked it free just in time. Then he put on an extra spurt and, with a few inches to spare, slipped through a hole in the hedge and was seen no more.

Silent and terrified, the animals crept back into the barn. In a moment the dogs came bounding back. At first no one had been able to imagine where these creatures came from, but the problem was soon solved: they were the puppies whom Napoleon had taken away from their mothers and reared privately. Though not yet full-grown, they were huge dogs, and as fierce-looking as wolves. They kept close to Napoleon. It was noticed that they wagged their tails to him in the same way as the other dogs had been used to do to Mr. Jones.

Napoleon, with the dogs following him, now mounted on to the raised portion of the floor where Major had previously stood to deliver his speech. He announced that from now on the Sunday-morning Meetings would come to an end. They were unnecessary, he said, and wasted time. In future all questions relating to the working of the farm would be settled by a special committee of pigs, presided over by himself. These would meet in private and

afterwards communicate their decisions to the others. The animals would still assemble on Sunday mornings to salute the flag, sing 'Beasts of England', and receive their orders for the week; but there would be no more debates.

In spite of the shock that Snowball's expulsion had given them, the animals were dismayed by this announcement. Several of them would have protested if they could have found the right arguments. Even Boxer was vaguely troubled. He set his ears back, shook his forelock several times, and tried hard to marshal his thoughts; but in the end he could not think of anything to say. Some of the pigs themselves, however, were more articulate. Four young porkers in the front row uttered shrill squeals of disapproval, and all four of them sprang to their feet and began speaking at once. But suddenly the dogs sitting round Napoleon let out deep, menacing growls, and the pigs fell silent and sat down again. Then the sheep broke out into a tremendous bleating of "Four legs good, two legs bad!" which went on for nearly a quarter of an hour and put an end to any chance of discussion.

Afterwards Squealer was sent round the farm to explain the new arrangement to the others.

"Comrades," he said, "I trust that every animal here appreciates the sacrifice that Comrade Napoleon has made in taking this extra labour upon himself. Do not imagine, comrades, that leadership is a pleasure! On the contrary, it is a deep and heavy responsibility. No one believes more firmly than Comrade Napoleon that all animals are equal. He would be only too happy to let you make your decisions for yourselves. But sometimes you might make the wrong decisions, comrades, and then where should we be? Suppose you had decided to follow Snowball, with his moonshine of windmills — Snowball, who, as we now know, was no better than a criminal?"

"He fought bravely at the Battle of the Cowshed," said somebody.

"Bravery is not enough," said Squealer. "Loyalty and obedience are more important. And as to the Battle of the Cowshed, I believe the time will come when we shall find that Snowball's part in it was much exaggerated. Discipline, comrades, iron discipline! That is the watchword for today. One false step, and our enemies would be upon us. Surely, comrades, you do not want Jones back?"

Once again this argument was unanswerable. Certainly the animals did not want Jones back; if the holding of debates on Sunday mornings was liable to bring him back, then the debates must stop. Boxer, who had now had time to think things over, voiced the general feeling by saying:

"If Comrade Napoleon says it, it must be right." And from then on he adopted the maxim, "Napoleon is always right," in addition to his private motto of "I will work harder."

By this time the weather had broken and the spring ploughing had begun. The shed where Snowball had drawn his plans of the windmill had been shut up and it was assumed that the plans had been rubbed off the floor. Every Sunday morning at ten o'clock the animals assembled in the big barn to receive their orders for the week. The skull of old Major, now clean of flesh, had been disinterred from the orchard and set up on a stump at the foot of the flagstaff, beside the gun. After the hoisting of the flag, the animals were required to file past the skull in a reverent manner before entering the barn. Nowadays they did not sit all together as they had done in the past. Napoleon, with Squealer and another pig named Minimus, who had a remarkable gift for composing songs and poems, sat on the front of the raised platform, with the nine young dogs forming a semicircle round them, and the other pigs sitting behind. The rest of the animals sat facing them in the main body of the barn. Napoleon read out the orders for the week in a gruff soldierly style, and after a single singing of 'Beasts of England', all the animals dispersed.

On the third Sunday after Snowball's expulsion, the animals were somewhat surprised to hear Napoleon announce that the windmill was to be built after all. He did not give any reason for having changed his mind, but merely warned the animals that this extra task would mean very hard work, it might even be necessary to reduce their rations. The plans, however, had all been prepared, down to the last detail. A special committee of pigs had been at work upon them for the past three weeks.

The building of the windmill, with various other improvements, was expected to take two years.

That evening Squealer explained privately to the other animals that Napoleon had never in reality been opposed to the windmill. On the contrary, it was he who had advocated it in the beginning, and the plan which Snowball had drawn on the floor of the incubator shed had actually been stolen from among Napoleon's papers. The windmill was, in fact, Napoleon's own creation. Why, then, asked somebody, had he spoken so strongly against it? Here Squealer looked very sly. That, he said, was Comrade Napoleon's cunning. He had SEEMED to oppose the windmill, simply as a manoeuvre to get rid of Snowball, who was a dangerous character and a bad influence. Now that Snowball was out of the way, the plan could go forward without his interference. This, said Squealer, was something called tactics. He repeated a number of times, "Tactics, comrades, tactics!" skipping round and whisking his tail with a merry laugh. The animals were not certain what the word meant, but Squealer spoke so persuasively, and the three dogs who happened to be with him growled so threateningly, that they accepted his explanation without further questions.

CHAPTER 6

All that year the animals worked like slaves. But they were happy in their work; they grudged no effort or sacrifice, well aware that everything that they did was for the benefit of themselves and those of their kind who would come after them, and not for a pack of idle, thieving human beings.

Throughout the spring and summer they worked a sixty-hour week, and in August Napoleon announced that there would be work on Sunday afternoons as well. This work was strictly voluntary, but any animal who absented himself from it would have his rations reduced by half. Even so, it was found necessary to leave certain tasks undone. The harvest was a little less successful than in the previous year, and two fields which should have been sown with roots in the early summer were not sown because the ploughing had not been completed early enough. It was possible to foresee that the coming winter would be a hard one.

The windmill presented unexpected difficulties. There

was a good quarry of limestone on the farm, and plenty of sand and cement had been found in one of the outhouses, so that all the materials for building were at hand. But the problem the animals could not at first solve was how to break up the stone into pieces of suitable size. There seemed no way of doing this except with picks and crowbars, which no animal could use, because no animal could stand on his hind legs. Only after weeks of vain effort did the right idea occur to somebody-namely, to utilise the force of gravity. Huge boulders, far too big to be used as they were, were lying all over the bed of the quarry. The animals lashed ropes round these, and then all together, cows, horses, sheep, any animal that could lay hold of the rope — even the pigs sometimes joined in at critical moments — they dragged them with desperate slowness up the slope to the top of the quarry, where they were toppled over the edge, to shatter to pieces below. Transporting the stone when it was once broken was comparatively simple. The horses carried it off in cart-loads, the sheep dragged single blocks, even Muriel and Benjamin yoked themselves into an old governess-cart and did their share. By late summer a sufficient store of stone had accumulated, and then the building began, under the superintendence of the pigs.

But it was a slow, laborious process. Frequently it took a whole day of exhausting effort to drag a single boulder to

the top of the quarry, and sometimes when it was pushed over the edge it failed to break. Nothing could have been achieved without Boxer, whose strength seemed equal to that of all the rest of the animals put together. When the boulder began to slip and the animals cried out in despair at finding themselves dragged down the hill, it was always Boxer who strained himself against the rope and brought the boulder to a stop. To see him toiling up the slope inch by inch, his breath coming fast, the tips of his hoofs clawing at the ground, and his great sides matted with sweat, filled everyone with admiration. Clover warned him sometimes to be careful not to overstrain himself, but Boxer would never listen to her. His two slogans, "I will work harder" and "Napoleon is always right," seemed to him a sufficient answer to all problems. He had made arrangements with the cockerel to call him three-quarters of an hour earlier in the mornings instead of half an hour. And in his spare moments, of which there were not many nowadays, he would go alone to the quarry, collect a load of broken stone, and drag it down to the site of the windmill unassisted.

The animals were not badly off throughout that summer, in spite of the hardness of their work. If they had no more food than they had had in Jones's day, at least they did not have less. The advantage of only having to feed themselves, and not having to support five extravagant human beings as well, was so great that it would have taken a lot of failures to outweigh it. And in many ways the animal method of doing things was more efficient and saved labour. Such jobs as weeding, for instance, could be done with a thoroughness impossible to human beings. And again, since no animal now stole, it was unnecessary to fence off pasture from arable land, which saved a lot of labour on the upkeep of hedges and gates. Nevertheless, as the summer wore on, various unforeseen shortages began to make themselves felt. There was need of paraffin oil, nails, string, dog biscuits, and iron for the horses' shoes, none of which could be produced on the farm. Later there would also be need for seeds and artificial manures, besides various tools and, finally, the machinery for the windmill. How these were to be procured, no one was able to imagine.

One Sunday morning, when the animals assembled to receive their orders, Napoleon announced that he had decided upon a new policy. From now onwards Animal Farm would engage in trade with the neighbouring farms: not, of course, for any commercial purpose, but simply in order to obtain certain materials which were urgently necessary. The needs of the windmill must override everything else, he said. He was therefore making arrangements to sell a stack of hay and part of the current year's wheat crop, and later on, if more money were

needed, it would have to be made up by the sale of eggs, for which there was always a market in Willingdon. The hens, said Napoleon, should welcome this sacrifice as their own special contribution towards the building of the windmill.

Once again the animals were conscious of a vague uneasiness. Never to have any dealings with human beings, never to engage in trade, never to make use of money — had not these been among the earliest resolutions passed at that first triumphant Meeting after Jones was expelled? All the animals remembered passing such resolutions: or at least they thought that they remembered it. The four young pigs who had protested when Napoleon abolished the Meetings raised their voices timidly, but they were promptly silenced by a tremendous growling from the dogs. Then, as usual, the sheep broke into "Four legs good, two legs bad!" and the momentary awkwardness was smoothed over. Finally Napoleon raised his trotter for silence and announced that he had already made all the arrangements. There would be no need for any of the animals to come in contact with human beings, which would clearly be most undesirable. He intended to take the whole burden upon his own shoulders. A Mr. Whymper, a solicitor living in Willingdon, had agreed to act as intermediary between Animal Farm and the outside world, and would visit the farm every Monday morning to receive his instructions.

Napoleon ended his speech with his usual cry of "Long live Animal Farm!" and after the singing of 'Beasts of England' the animals were dismissed.

Afterwards Squealer made a round of the farm and set the animals' minds at rest. He assured them that the resolution against engaging in trade and using money had never been passed, or even suggested. It was pure imagination, probably traceable in the beginning to lies circulated by Snowball. A few animals still felt faintly doubtful, but Squealer asked them shrewdly, "Are you certain that this is not something that you have dreamed, comrades? Have you any record of such a resolution? Is it written down anywhere?" And since it was certainly true that nothing of the kind existed in writing, the animals were satisfied that they had been mistaken.

Every Monday Mr. Whymper visited the farm as had been arranged. He was a sly-looking little man with side whiskers, a solicitor in a very small way of business, but sharp enough to have realised earlier than anyone else that Animal Farm would need a broker and that the commissions would be worth having.

The animals watched his coming and going with a kind of dread, and avoided him as much as possible. Nevertheless, the sight of Napoleon, on all fours, delivering orders to Whymper, who stood on two legs, roused their pride and partly reconciled them to the new arrangement.

Their relations with the human race were now not quite the same as they had been before. The human beings did not hate Animal Farm any less now that it was prospering; indeed, they hated it more than ever. Every human being held it as an article of faith that the farm would go bankrupt sooner or later, and, above all, that the windmill would be a failure. They would meet in the public-houses and prove to one another by means of diagrams that the windmill was bound to fall down, or that if it did stand up, then that it would never work. And yet, against their will, they had developed a certain respect for the efficiency with which the animals were managing their own affairs. One symptom of this was that they had begun to call Animal Farm by its proper name and ceased to pretend that it was called the Manor Farm. They had also dropped their championship of Jones, who had given up hope of getting his farm back and gone to live in another part of the county. Except through Whymper, there was as yet no contact between Animal Farm and the outside world, but there were constant rumours that Napoleon was about to enter into a definite business agreement either with Mr. Pilkington of Foxwood or with Mr. Frederick of Pinchfield — but never, it was noticed, with both simultaneously.

It was about this time that the pigs suddenly moved into the farmhouse and took up their residence there. Again the animals seemed to remember that a resolution against this had been passed in the early days, and again Squealer was able to convince them that this was not the case. It was absolutely necessary, he said, that the pigs, who were the brains of the farm, should have a quiet place to work in. It was also more suited to the dignity of the Leader (for of late he had taken to speaking of Napoleon under the title of "Leader") to live in a house than in a mere sty. Nevertheless, some of the animals were disturbed when they heard that the pigs not only took their meals in the kitchen and used the drawing-room as a recreation room, but also slept in the beds. Boxer passed it off as

usual with "Napoleon is always right!" , but Clover, who thought she remembered a definite ruling against beds, went to the end of the barn and tried to puzzle out the Seven Commandments which were inscribed there. Finding herself unable to read more than individual letters, she fetched Muriel.

"Muriel," she said, "read me the Fourth Commandment. Does it not say something about never sleeping in a bed?"

With some difficulty Muriel spelt it out.

"It says, 'No animal shall sleep in a bed with sheets,' " she announced finally.

Curiously enough, Clover had not remembered that the Fourth Commandment mentioned sheets; but as it was there on the wall, it must have done so. And Squealer, who happened to be passing at this moment, attended by two or three dogs, was able to put the whole matter in its proper perspective.

"You have heard then, comrades," he said, "that we pigs now sleep in the beds of the farmhouse? And why not? You did not suppose, surely, that there was ever a ruling against beds? A bed merely means a place to sleep in. A pile of straw in a stall is a bed, properly regarded. The rule was against sheets, which are a human invention. We have removed the sheets from the farmhouse beds, and sleep between blankets. And very comfortable beds they are too! But not more comfortable than we need, I can tell you, comrades, with all the brainwork we have to do nowadays.

You would not rob us of our repose, would you, comrades? You would not have us too tired to carry out our duties? Surely none of you wishes to see Jones back?"

The animals reassured him on this point immediately, and no more was said about the pigs sleeping in the farmhouse beds. And when, some days afterwards, it was announced that from now on the pigs would get up an hour later in the mornings than the other animals, no complaint was made about that either.

By the autumn the animals were tired but happy. They had had a hard year, and after the sale of part of the hay and corn, the stores of food for the winter were none too plentiful, but the windmill compensated for everything. It was almost half built now. After the harvest there was a stretch of clear dry weather, and the animals toiled harder than ever, thinking it well worth while to plod to and fro all day with blocks of stone if by doing so they could raise the walls another foot. Boxer would even come out at nights and work for an hour or two on his own by the light of the harvest moon. In their spare moments the animals would walk round and round the half-finished mill, admiring the strength and perpendicularity of its walls and marvelling that they should ever have been able to build anything so

imposing. Only old Benjamin refused to grow enthusiastic about the windmill, though, as usual, he would utter nothing beyond the cryptic remark that donkeys live a long time.

November came, with raging south-west winds. Building had to stop because it was now too wet to mix the cement. Finally there came a night when the gale was so violent that the farm buildings rocked on their foundations and several tiles were blown off the roof of the barn. The hens woke up squawking with terror because they had all dreamed simultaneously of hearing a gun go off in the distance. In the morning the animals came out of their stalls to find that the flagstaff had been blown down and an elm tree at the foot of the orchard had been plucked up like a radish. They had just noticed this when a cry of despair broke from every animal's throat. A terrible sight had met their eyes. The windmill was in ruins.

With one accord they dashed down to the spot. Napoleon, who seldom moved out of a walk, raced ahead of them all. Yes, there it lay, the fruit of all their struggles, levelled to its foundations, the stones they had broken and carried so laboriously scattered all around. Unable at first to speak, they stood gazing mournfully at the litter of fallen stone. Napoleon paced to and fro in silence, occasionally snuffing at the ground. His tail had grown rigid and twitched sharply from side to side, a sign in him of intense mental activity. Suddenly he halted as though his mind were made up.

"Comrades," he said quietly, "do you know who is responsible for this? Do you know the enemy who has come in the night and overthrown our windmill? SNOWBALL!" he suddenly roared in a voice of thunder. "Snowball has done this thing! In sheer malignity, thinking to set back our plans and avenge himself for his ignominious expulsion, this traitor has crept here under cover of night and destroyed our work of nearly a year. Comrades, here and now I pronounce the death sentence upon Snowball. 'Animal Hero, Second Class,' and half a bushel of apples to any animal who brings him to justice. A full bushel to anyone who captures him alive!"

The animals were shocked beyond measure to learn that even Snowball could be guilty of such an action. There was a cry of indignation, and everyone began thinking out ways of catching Snowball if he should ever come back. Almost immediately the footprints of a pig were discovered in the grass at a little distance from the knoll. They could only be traced for a few yards, but appeared to lead to a hole in the hedge. Napoleon snuffed deeply at them and pronounced them to be Snowball's. He gave it as his opinion that Snowball had probably come from the direction of Foxwood Farm.

"No more delays, comrades!" cried Napoleon when

the footprints had been examined. "There is work to be done. This very morning we begin rebuilding the windmill, and we will build all through the winter, rain or shine. We will teach this miserable traitor that he cannot undo our work so easily. Remember, comrades, there must be no alteration in our plans: they shall be carried out to the day. Forward, comrades! Long live the windmill! Long live Animal Farm!"

CHAPTER 7

It was a bitter winter. The stormy weather was followed by sleet and snow, and then by a hard frost which did not break till well into February. The animals carried on as best they could with the rebuilding of the windmill, well knowing that the outside world was watching them and that the envious human beings would rejoice and triumph if the mill were not finished on time.

Out of spite, the human beings pretended not to believe that it was Snowball who had destroyer the windmill: they said that it had fallen down because the walls were too thin. The animals knew that this was not the case. Still, it had been decided to build the walls three feet thick this time instead of eighteen inches as before, which meant collecting much larger quantities of stone. For a long time the quarry was full of snowdrifts and nothing could be done. Some progress was made in the dry frosty weather that followed, but it was cruel work, and the animals could not feel so hopeful about it as they had felt before. They were always cold, and usually hungry as well. Only Boxer and Clover never lost heart. Squealer made excellent speeches on the joy of service and the dignity of labour, but the other animals found more inspiration in Boxer's strength and his never-failing cry of "I will work harder!"

In January food fell short. The corn ration was drastically reduced, and it was announced that an extra potato ration would be issued to make up for it. Then it was discovered that the greater part of the potato crop had been frosted in the clamps, which had not been covered thickly enough. The potatoes had become soft and discoloured, and only a few were edible. For days at a time the animals had nothing to eat but chaff and mangels. Starvation seemed to stare them in the face.

It was vitally necessary to conceal this fact from the outside world. Emboldened by the collapse of the windmill, the human beings were inventing fresh lies about Animal Farm. Once again it was being put about that all the animals were dying of famine and disease, and that they were continually fighting among themselves and had resorted to cannibalism and infanticide. Napoleon was well aware of the bad results that might follow if the real facts of the food situation were known, and he decided to make use of Mr. Whymper to spread a contrary impression. Hitherto the animals had had little or no contact with Whymper on his weekly visits: now, however, a few selected animals, mostly sheep, were instructed to remark casually in his hearing that rations had been increased. In addition, Napoleon ordered the almost empty bins in the store-shed to be filled nearly to the brim with sand, which was then covered up with what remained of the grain and meal. On some suitable pretext Whymper was led through the store-shed and allowed to catch a glimpse of the bins. He was deceived, and continued to report to the outside world that there was no food shortage on Animal Farm.

Nevertheless, towards the end of January it became obvious that it would be necessary to procure some more grain from somewhere. In these days Napoleon rarely appeared in public, but spent all his time in the farmhouse, which was guarded at each door by fierce-looking dogs.

When he did emerge, it was in a ceremonial manner, with an escort of six dogs who closely surrounded him and growled if anyone came too near.

Frequently he did not even appear on Sunday mornings, but issued his orders through one of the other pigs, usually Squealer.

One Sunday morning Squealer announced that the hens, who had just come in to lay again, must surrender their eggs. Napoleon had accepted, through Whymper, a contract for four hundred eggs a week. The price of these would pay for enough grain and meal to keep the farm going till summer came on and conditions were easier.

When the hens heard this, they raised a terrible outcry. They had been warned earlier that this sacrifice might be necessary, but had not believed that it would really happen. They were just getting their clutches ready for the spring sitting, and they protested that to take the eggs away now was murder. For the first time since the expulsion of Jones, there was something resembling a rebellion. Led by three young Black Minorca pullets, the hens made a determined effort to thwart Napoleon's wishes. Their method was to fly up to the rafters and there lay their eggs, which smashed to pieces on the floor. Napoleon acted swiftly and ruthlessly. He ordered the hens' rations to be stopped, and decreed that any animal giving so much as a grain of corn to a hen should be punished by death. The dogs saw to it that these orders were carried out. For five days the hens held out, then they capitulated and went back to their nesting boxes. Nine hens had died in the meantime. Their bodies were buried in the orchard, and it was given out that they had died of coccidiosis. Whymper heard nothing of this affair, and the eggs were duly delivered, a grocer's van driving up to the farm once a week to take them away.

All this while no more had been seen of Snowball. He was rumoured to be hiding on one of the neighbouring farms, either Foxwood or Pinchfield. Napoleon was by this time on slightly better terms with the other farmers than before. It happened that there was in the yard a pile of

timber which had been stacked there ten years earlier when a beech spinney was cleared. It was well seasoned, and Whymper had advised Napoleon to sell it; both Mr. Pilkington and Mr. Frederick were anxious to buy it. Napoleon was hesitating between the two, unable to make up his mind. It was noticed that whenever he seemed on the point of coming to an agreement with Frederick, Snowball was declared to be in hiding at Foxwood, while, when he inclined toward Pilkington, Snowball was said to be at Pinchfield.

Suddenly, early in the spring, an alarming thing was discovered. Snowball was secretly frequenting the farm by night! The animals were so disturbed that they could hardly sleep in their stalls. Every night, it was said, he came creeping in under cover of darkness and performed all kinds of mischief. He stole the corn, he upset the milk-pails, he broke the eggs, he trampled the seedbeds, he gnawed the bark off the fruit trees.

Whenever anything went wrong it became usual to attribute it to Snowball. If a window was broken or a drain was blocked up, someone was certain to say that Snowball had come in the night and done it, and when the key of the store-shed was lost, the whole farm was convinced that Snowball had thrown it down the well. Curiously enough, they went on believing this even after the mislaid key was found under a sack of meal. The cows declared unanimously that Snowball crept into their stalls and milked them in their sleep. The rats, which had been troublesome that winter, were also said to be in league with Snowball.

Napoleon decreed that there should be a full investigation into Snowball's activities. With his dogs in attendance he set out and made a careful tour of inspection of the farm buildings, the other animals following at a respectful distance. At every few steps Napoleon stopped and snuffed the ground for traces of Snowball's footsteps, which, he said, he could detect by the smell. He snuffed in every corner, in the barn, in the cow-shed, in the henhouses, in the vegetable garden, and found traces of Snowball almost everywhere. He would put his snout to the ground, give several deep sniffs, ad exclaim in a terrible voice, "Snowball! He has been here! I can smell him distinctly!" and at the word "Snowball" all the dogs let out blood-curdling growls and showed their side teeth.

The animals were thoroughly frightened. It seemed to them as though Snowball were some kind of invisible influence, pervading the air about them and menacing them with all kinds of dangers. In the evening Squealer called them together, and with an alarmed expression on his face told them that he had some serious news to report.

"Comrades!" cried Squealer, making little nervous skips, "a most terrible thing has been discovered.

Snowball has sold himself to Frederick of Pinchfield Farm, who is even now plotting to attack us and take our farm away from us! Snowball is to act as his guide when the attack begins. But there is worse than that. We had thought that Snowball's rebellion was caused simply by his vanity and ambition. But we were wrong, comrades. Do you know what the real reason was? Snowball was in league with Jones from the very start! He was Jones's secret agent all the time. It has all been proved by documents which he left behind him and which we have only just discovered. To my mind this explains a great deal, comrades. Did we not see for ourselves how he attempted — fortunately without success — to get us defeated and destroyed at the Battle of the Cowshed?"

The animals were stupefied. This was a wickedness far outdoing Snowball's destruction of the windmill. But it was some minutes before they could fully take it in. They all remembered, or thought they remembered, how they had seen Snowball charging ahead of them at the Battle of the Cowshed, how he had rallied and encouraged them at every turn, and how he had not paused for an instant even when the pellets from Jones's gun had wounded his back. At first it was a little difficult to see how this fitted in with his being on Jones's side. Even Boxer, who seldom asked questions, was puzzled. He lay down, tucked his fore hoofs beneath him, shut his eyes, and with a hard effort managed to formulate his thoughts.

"I do not believe that," he said. "Snowball fought bravely at the Battle of the Cowshed. I saw him myself. Did we not give him 'Animal Hero, first Class,' immediately afterwards?"

"That was our mistake, comrade. For we know now — it is all written down in the secret documents that we have found — that in reality he was trying to lure us to our doom."

"But he was wounded," said Boxer. "We all saw him running with blood."

"That was part of the arrangement!" cried Squealer. "Jones's shot only grazed him. I could show you this in his own writing, if you were able to read it. The plot was for Snowball, at the critical moment, to give the signal for flight and leave the field to the enemy. And he very nearly succeeded — I will even say, comrades, he WOULD have succeeded if it had not been for our heroic Leader, Comrade Napoleon. Do you not remember how, just at the moment when Jones and his men had got inside the yard, Snowball suddenly turned and fled, and many animals followed him? And do you not remember, too, that it was just at that moment, when panic was spreading and all seemed lost, that Comrade Napoleon sprang forward with a cry of 'Death to Humanity!' and sank his teeth in Jones's leg? Surely you remember THAT, comrades?"

exclaimed Squealer, frisking from side to side.

Now when Squealer described the scene so graphically, it seemed to the animals that they did remember it. At any rate, they remembered that at the critical moment of the battle Snowball had turned to flee. But Boxer was still a little uneasy.

"I do not believe that Snowball was a traitor at the beginning," he said finally. "What he has done since is different. But I believe that at the Battle of the Cowshed he was a good comrade."

"Our Leader, Comrade Napoleon," announced Squealer, speaking very slowly and firmly, "has stated categorically — categorically, comrade — that Snowball was Jones's agent from the very beginning — yes, and from long before the Rebellion was ever thought of."

"Ah, that is different!" said Boxer. "If Comrade Napoleon says it, it must be right."

"That is the true spirit, comrade!" cried Squealer, but it was noticed he cast a very ugly look at Boxer with his little twinkling eyes. He turned to go, then paused and added impressively: "I warn every animal on this farm to keep his eyes very wide open. For we have reason to think that some of Snowball's secret agents are lurking among us at this moment!"

Four days later, in the late afternoon, Napoleon ordered all the animals to assemble in the yard. When they

were all gathered together, Napoleon emerged from the farmhouse, wearing both his medals (for he had recently awarded himself "Animal Hero, First Class", and "Animal Hero, Second Class"), with his nine huge dogs frisking round him and uttering growls that sent shivers down all the animals' spines. They all cowered silently in their places, seeming to know in advance that some terrible thing was about to happen.

Napoleon stood sternly surveying his audience; then he uttered a high-pitched whimper. Immediately the dogs bounded forward, seized four of the pigs by the ear and dragged them, squealing with pain and terror, to Napoleon's feet. The pigs' ears were bleeding, the dogs had tasted blood, and for a few moments they appeared to go quite mad. To the amazement of everybody, three of them flung themselves upon Boxer.

Boxer saw them coming and put out his great hoof, caught a dog in mid-air, and pinned him to the ground. The dog shrieked for mercy and the other two fled with their tails between their legs. Boxer looked at Napoleon to know whether he should crush the dog to death or let it go. Napoleon appeared to change countenance, and sharply ordered Boxer to let the dog go, whereat Boxer lifted his hoof, and the dog slunk away, bruised and howling.

Presently the tumult died down. The four pigs waited, trembling, with guilt written on every line of their

countenances. Napoleon now called upon them to confess their crimes. They were the same four pigs as had protested when Napoleon abolished the Sunday Meetings. Without any further prompting they confessed that they had been secretly in touch with Snowball ever since his expulsion, that they had collaborated with him in destroying the windmill, and that they had entered into an agreement with him to hand over Animal Farm to Mr. Frederick. They added that Snowball had privately admitted to them that he had been Jones's secret agent for years past. When they had finished their confession, the dogs promptly tore their throats out, and in a terrible voice Napoleon demanded whether any other animal had anything to confess.

The three hens who had been the ringleaders in the attempted rebellion over the eggs now came forward and stated that Snowball had appeared to them in a dream and incited them to disobey Napoleon's orders. They, too, were slaughtered. Then a goose came forward and confessed to having secreted six ears of corn during the last year's harvest and eaten them in the night. Then a sheep confessed to having urinated in the drinking pool — urged to do this, so she said, by Snowball — and two other sheep confessed to having murdered an old ram, an especially devoted follower of Napoleon, by chasing him round and round a bonfire when he was suffering from a cough. They were all slain on the spot. And so the tale of confessions

and executions went on, until there was a pile of corpses lying before Napoleon's feet and the air was heavy with the smell of blood, which had been unknown there since the expulsion of Jones.

When it was all over, the remaining animals, except for the pigs and dogs, crept away in a body. They were shaken and miserable. They did not know which was more shocking — the treachery of the animals who had leagued themselves with Snowball, or the cruel retribution they had just witnessed. In the old days there had often been scenes of bloodshed equally terrible, but it seemed to all of them that it was far worse now that it was happening among themselves. Since Jones had left the farm, until today, no animal had killed another animal. Not even a rat had been killed. They had made their way on to the little knoll where the half-finished windmill stood, and with one accord they all lay down as though huddling together for warmth — Clover, Muriel, Benjamin, the cows, the sheep, and a whole flock of geese and hens — everyone, indeed, except the cat, who had suddenly disappeared just before Napoleon ordered the animals to assemble. For some time nobody spoke. Only Boxer remained on his feet. He fidgeted to and fro, swishing his long black tail against his sides and occasionally uttering a little whinny of surprise. Finally he said:

"I do not understand it. I would not have believed

that such things could happen on our farm. It must be due to some fault in ourselves. The solution, as I see it, is to work harder. From now onwards I shall get up a full hour earlier in the mornings."

And he moved off at his lumbering trot and made for the quarry. Having got there, he collected two successive loads of stone and dragged them down to the windmill before retiring for the night.

The animals huddled about Clover, not speaking. The knoll where they were lying gave them a wide prospect across the countryside. Most of Animal Farm was within their view — the long pasture stretching down to the main road, the hayfield, the spinney, the drinking pool, the ploughed fields where the young wheat was thick and green, and the red roofs of the farm buildings with the smoke curling from the chimneys. It was a clear spring evening. The grass and the bursting hedges were gilded by the level rays of the sun. Never had the farm — and with a kind of surprise they remembered that it was their own farm, every inch of it their own property — appeared to the animals so desirable a place. As Clover looked down the hillside her eyes filled with tears. If she could have spoken her thoughts, it would have been to say that this was not what they had aimed at when they had set themselves years ago to work for the overthrow of the human race.

These scenes of terror and slaughter were not what

they had looked forward to on that night when old Major first stirred them to rebellion. If she herself had had any picture of the future, it had been of a society of animals set free from hunger and the whip, all equal, each working according to his capacity, the strong protecting the weak, as she had protected the lost brood of ducklings with her foreleg on the night of Major's speech.

Instead — she did not know why — they had come to a time when no one dared speak his mind, when fierce, growling dogs roamed everywhere, and when you had to watch your comrades torn to pieces after confessing to shocking crimes.

There was no thought of rebellion or disobedience in her mind. She knew that, even as things were, they were far better off than they had been in the days of Jones, and that before all else it was needful to prevent the return of the human beings. Whatever happened she would remain faithful, work hard, carry out the orders that were given to her, and accept the leadership of Napoleon. But still, it was not for this that she and all the other animals had hoped and toiled. It was not for this that they had built the windmill and faced the bullets of Jones's gun. Such were her thoughts, though she lacked the words to express them.

At last, feeling this to be in some way a substitute for the words she was unable to find, she began to sing 'Beasts of England'. The other animals sitting round

her took it up, and they sang it three times over — very tunefully, but slowly and mournfully, in a way they had never sung it before.

They had just finished singing it for the third time when Squealer, attended by two dogs, approached them with the air of having something important to say. He announced that, by a special decree of Comrade Napoleon, 'Beasts of England' had been abolished. From now onwards it was forbidden to sing it.

The animals were taken aback. "Why?" cried Muriel.

"It's no longer needed, comrade," said Squealer stiffly. " 'Beasts of England' was the song of the Rebellion. But the Rebellion is now completed. The execution of the traitors this afternoon was the final act. The enemy both external and internal has been defeated. In 'Beasts of England' we expressed our longing for a better society in days to come. But that society has now been established. Clearly this song has no longer any purpose."

Frightened though they were, some of the animals might possibly have protested, but at this moment the sheep set up their usual bleating of "Four legs good, two legs bad," which went on for several minutes and put an end to the discussion.

So 'Beasts of England' was heard no more. In its place Minimus, the poet, had composed another song which began:

Animal Farm, Animal Farm,
Never through me shalt thou come to harm!

And this was sung every Sunday morning after the hoisting of the flag. But somehow neither the words nor the tune ever seemed to the animals to come up to ' Beasts of England ' .

CHAPTER 8

A few days later, when the terror caused by the executions had died down, some of the animals remembered — or thought they remembered — that the Sixth Commandment decreed "No animal shall kill any other animal." And though no one cared to mention it in the hearing of the pigs or the dogs, it was felt that the killings which had taken place did not square with this. Clover asked Benjamin to read her the Sixth Commandment, and when Benjamin, as usual, said that he refused to meddle in such matters, she fetched Muriel. Muriel read the Commandment for her. It ran: "No animal shall kill any other animal WITHOUT CAUSE." Somehow or other, the last two words had slipped out of the animals' memory. But they saw now that the Commandment had not been violated; for clearly there was good reason for killing the traitors who had leagued themselves with Snowball.

Throughout the year the animals worked even harder than they had worked in the previous year. To rebuild the

windmill, with walls twice as thick as before, and to finish it by the appointed date, together with the regular work of the farm, was a tremendous labour. There were times when it seemed to the animals that they worked longer hours and fed no better than they had done in Jones's day.

On Sunday mornings Squealer, holding down a long strip of paper with his trotter, would read out to them lists of figures proving that the production of every class of foodstuff had increased by two hundred per cent, three hundred per cent, or five hundred per cent, as the case might be. The animals saw no reason to disbelieve him,

especially as they could no longer remember very clearly what conditions had been like before the Rebellion. All the same, there were days when they felt that they would sooner have had less figures and more food.

All orders were now issued through Squealer or one of the other pigs. Napoleon himself was not seen in public as often as once in a fortnight. When he did appear, he was attended not only by his retinue of dogs but by a black cockerel who marched in front of him and acted as a kind of trumpeter, letting out a loud "cock-a-doodle-doo" before Napoleon spoke. Even in the farmhouse, it was said, Napoleon inhabited separate apartments from the others. He took his meals alone, with two dogs to wait upon him, and always ate from the Crown Derby dinner service which had been in the glass cupboard in the drawing-room. It was also announced that the gun would be fired every year on Napoleon's birthday, as well as on the other two anniversaries.

Napoleon was now never spoken of simply as "Napoleon." He was always referred to in formal style as "our Leader, Comrade Napoleon," and this pigs liked to invent for him such titles as Father of All Animals, Terror of Mankind, Protector of the Sheep-fold, Ducklings' Friend, and the like. In his speeches, Squealer would talk with the tears rolling down his cheeks of Napoleon's wisdom the goodness of his heart, and the

deep love he bore to all animals everywhere, even and especially the unhappy animals who still lived in ignorance and slavery on other farms. It had become usual to give Napoleon the credit for every successful achievement and every stroke of good fortune. You would often hear one hen remark to another, "Under the guidance of our Leader, Comrade Napoleon, I have laid five eggs in six days"; or two cows, enjoying a drink at the pool, would exclaim, "Thanks to the leadership of Comrade Napoleon, how excellent this water tastes!" The general feeling on the farm was well expressed in a poem entitled Comrade Napoleon, which was composed by Minimus and which ran as follows:

Friend of fatherless!
Fountain of happiness!
Lord of the swill-bucket! Oh, how my soul is on
Fire when I gaze at thy
Calm and commanding eye,
Like the sun in the sky,
Comrade Napoleon!

Thou are the giver of
All that thy creatures love,
Full belly twice a day, clean straw to roll upon;
Every beast great or small
Sleeps at peace in his stall,
Thou watchest over all,
Comrade Napoleon!

Had I a sucking-pig,
Ere he had grown as big
Even as a pint bottle or as a rolling-pin,
He should have learned to be
Faithful and true to thee,
Yes, his first squeak should be
"Comrade Napoleon!"

Napoleon approved of this poem and caused it to be inscribed on the wall of the big barn, at the opposite end from the Seven Commandments. It was surmounted by a portrait of Napoleon, in profile, executed by Squealer in white paint.

Meanwhile, through the agency of Whymper, Napoleon was engaged in complicated negotiations with Frederick and Pilkington. The pile of timber was still unsold. Of the two, Frederick was the more anxious to get hold of it, but he would not offer a reasonable price. At the same time there were renewed rumours that Frederick and his men were plotting to attack Animal Farm and to destroy the windmill, the building of which had aroused furious jealousy in him. Snowball was known to be still skulking on Pinchfield Farm. In the middle of the summer the animals were alarmed to hear that three hens had come forward and confessed that, inspired by Snowball, they had entered into a plot to murder Napoleon. They were executed immediately, and fresh precautions for Napoleon's safety were taken. Four dogs guarded his bed at night, one at each corner, and a young pig named Pinkeye was given the task of tasting all his food before he ate it, lest it should be poisoned.

At about the same time it was given out that Napoleon had arranged to sell the pile of timber to Mr. Pilkington; he was also going to enter into a regular agreement for the exchange of certain products between Animal Farm and Foxwood. The relations between Napoleon and Pilkington, though they were only conducted through Whymper, were now almost friendly. The animals distrusted Pilkington, as a human being, but greatly preferred him to Frederick, whom

they both feared and hated. As the summer wore on, and the windmill neared completion, the rumours of an impending treacherous attack grew stronger and stronger.

Frederick, it was said, intended to bring against them twenty men all armed with guns, and he had already bribed the magistrates and police, so that if he could once get hold of the title-deeds of Animal Farm they would ask no questions. Moreover, terrible stories were leaking out from Pinchfield about the cruelties that Frederick practised upon his animals. He had flogged an old horse to death, he starved his cows, he had killed a dog by throwing it into the furnace, he amused himself in the evenings by making cocks fight with splinters of razor-blade tied to their spurs.

The animals' blood boiled with rage when they heard of these things beingdone to their comrades, and sometimes they clamoured to be allowed to go out in a body and attack Pinchfield Farm, drive out the humans, and set the animals free. But Squealer counselled them to avoid rash actions and trust in Comrade Napoleon's strategy.

Nevertheless, feeling against Frederick continued to run high. One Sunday morning Napoleon appeared in the barn and explained that he had never at any time contemplated selling the pile of timber to Frederick; he considered it beneath his dignity, he said, to have dealings with scoundrels of that description. The pigeons who were still sent out to spread tidings of the Rebellion were forbidden to set foot anywhere on Foxwood, and were also ordered to drop their former slogan of "Death to Humanity" in favour of "Death to Frederick." In the late summer yet another of Snowball's machinations was laid bare. The wheat crop was full of weeds, and it was discovered that on one of his nocturnal visits Snowball had mixed weed seeds with the seed corn. A gander who had been privy to the plot had confessed his guilt to Squealer and immediately committed suicide by swallowing deadly nightshade berries. The animals now also learned that Snowball had never — as many of them had believed hitherto — received the order of "Animal Hero, First Class." This was merely a legend which had been spread some time after the Battle of the Cowshed by Snowball himself. So far from being decorated, he had been censured for showing cowardice in the battle. Once again some of the animals heard this with a certain bewilderment, but Squealer was soon able to convince them that their memories had been at fault.

In the autumn, by a tremendous, exhausting effort — for the harvest had to be gathered at almost the same time — the windmill was finished. The machinery had still to be installed, and Whymper was negotiating the purchase of it, but the structure was completed. In the teeth of every difficulty, in spite of inexperience, of primitive implements,

of bad luck and of Snowball's treachery, the work had been finished punctually to the very day! Tired out but proud, the animals walked round and round their masterpiece, which appeared even more beautiful in their eyes than when it had been built the first time. Moreover, the walls were twice as thick as before. Nothing short of explosives would lay them low this time! And when they thought of how they had laboured, what discouragements they had overcome, and the enormous difference that would be made in their lives when the sails were turning and the dynamos running — when they thought of all this, their tiredness forsook them and they gambolled round and round the windmill, uttering cries of triumph. Napoleon himself, attended by his dogs and his cockerel, came down to inspect the completed work; he personally congratulated the animals on their achievement, and announced that the mill would be named Napoleon Mill.

Two days later the animals were called together for a special meeting in the barn. They were struck dumb with

surprise when Napoleon announced that he had sold the pile of timber to Frederick. Tomorrow Frederick's wagons would arrive and begin carting it away. Throughout the whole period of his seeming friendship with Pilkington, Napoleon had really been in secret agreement with Frederick.

All relations with Foxwood had been broken off; insulting messages had been sent to Pilkington. The pigeons had been told to avoid Pinchfield Farm and to alter their slogan from "Death to Frederick" to "Death to Pilkington." At the same time Napoleon assured the animals that the stories of an impending attack on Animal Farm were completely untrue, and that the tales about Frederick's cruelty to his own animals had been greatly exaggerated. All these rumours had probably originated with Snowball and his agents. It now appeared that Snowball was not, after all, hiding on Pinchfield Farm, and in fact had never been there in his life: he was living — in considerable luxury, so it was said — at Foxwood, and had in reality been a pensioner of Pilkington for years past.

The pigs were in ecstasies over Napoleon's cunning. By seeming to be friendly with Pilkington he had forced Frederick to raise his price by twelve pounds. But the superior quality of Napoleon's mind, said Squealer, was shown in the fact that he trusted nobody, not even Frederick. Frederick had wanted to pay for the timber with

something called a cheque, which, it seemed, was a piece of paper with a promise to pay written upon it. But Napoleon was too clever for him. He had demanded payment in real five-pound notes, which were to be handed over before the timber was removed. Already Frederick had paid up; and the sum he had paid was just enough to buy the machinery for the windmill.

Meanwhile the timber was being carted away at high speed. When it was all gone, another special meeting was held in the barn for the animals to inspect Frederick's bank-notes. Smiling beatifically, and wearing both his decorations, Napoleon reposed on a bed of straw on the platform, with the money at his side, neatly piled on a china dish from the farmhouse kitchen. The animals filed slowly past, and each gazed his fill. And Boxer put out his nose to sniff at the bank-notes, and the flimsy white things stirred and rustled in his breath.

Three days later there was a terrible hullabaloo. Whymper, his face deadly pale, came racing up the path on his bicycle, flung it down in the yard and rushed straight into the farmhouse. The next moment a choking roar of rage sounded from Napoleon's apartments. The news of what had happened sped round the farm like wildfire. The banknotes were forgeries! Frederick had got the timber for nothing!

Napoleon called the animals together immediately and

in a terrible voice pronounced the death sentence upon Frederick. When captured, he said, Frederick should be boiled alive. At the same time he warned them that after this treacherous deed the worst was to be expected. Frederick and his men might make their long-expected attack at any moment. Sentinels were placed at all the approaches to the farm. In addition, four pigeons were sent to Foxwood with a conciliatory message, which it was hoped might re-establish good relations with Pilkington.

The very next morning the attack came. The animals were at breakfast when the look-outs came racing in with the news that Frederick and his followers had already come through the five-barred gate. Boldly enough the animals sallied forth to meet them, but this time they did not have the easy victory that they had had in the Battle of the Cowshed. There were fifteen men, with half a dozen guns between them, and they opened fire as soon as they got within fifty yards. The animals could not face the terrible explosions and the stinging pellets, and in spite of the efforts of Napoleon and Boxer to rally them, they were soon driven back. A number of them were already wounded. They took refuge in the farm buildings and peeped cautiously out from chinks and knot-holes. The whole of the big pasture, including the windmill, was in the hands of the enemy. For the moment even Napoleon seemed at a loss. He paced up and down without a word,

his tail rigid and twitching. Wistful glances were sent in the direction of Foxwood. If Pilkington and his men would help them, the day might yet be won. But at this moment the four pigeons, who had been sent out on the day before, returned, one of them bearing a scrap of paper from Pilkington. On it was pencilled the words: "Serves you right."

Meanwhile Frederick and his men had halted about the windmill. The animals watched them, and a murmur of dismay went round. Two of the men had produced a crowbar and a sledge hammer. They were going to knock the windmill down.

"Impossible!" cried Napoleon. "We have built the walls far too thick for that. They could not knock it down in a week. Courage, comrades!"

But Benjamin was watching the movements of the men intently. The two with the hammer and the crowbar were drilling a hole near the base of the windmill. Slowly, and with an air almost of amusement, Benjamin nodded his long muzzle.

"I thought so," he said. "Do you not see what they are doing? In another moment they are going to pack blasting powder into that hole."

Terrified, the animals waited. It was impossible now to venture out of the shelter of the buildings. After a few minutes the men were seen to be running in all directions.

Then there was a deafening roar. The pigeons swirled into the air, and all the animals, except Napoleon, flung themselves flat on their bellies and hid their faces. When they got up again, a huge cloud of black smoke was hanging where the windmill had been. Slowly the breeze drifted it away. The windmill had ceased to exist!

At this sight the animals' courage returned to them. The fear and despair they had felt a moment earlier were drowned in their rage against this vile, contemptible act. A mighty cry for vengeance went up, and without waiting for further orders they charged forth in a body and made straight for the enemy. This time they did not heed the cruel pellets that swept over them like hail. It was a savage, bitter battle. The men fired again and again, and, when the animals got to close quarters, lashed out with their sticks and their heavy boots. A cow, three sheep, and two geese were killed, and nearly everyone was wounded. Even Napoleon, who was directing operations from the rear, had the tip of his tail chipped by a pellet. But the men did not go unscathed either. Three of them had their heads broken by blows from Boxer's hoofs; another was gored in the belly by a cow's horn; another had his trousers nearly torn off by Jessie and Bluebell. And when the nine dogs of Napoleon's own bodyguard, whom he had instructed to make a detour under cover of the hedge, suddenly appeared on the men's flank, baying ferociously, panic overtook them. They saw that they were in danger of being surrounded. Frederick shouted to his men to get out while the going was good, and the next moment the cowardly enemy was running for dear life. The animals chased them right down to the bottom of the field, and got in some last kicks at them as they forced their way through the thorn hedge.

They had won, but they were weary and bleeding. Slowly they began to limp back towards the farm. The sight of their dead comrades stretched upon the grass moved some of them to tears. And for a little while they halted in sorrowful silence at the place where the windmill had once stood. Yes, it was gone; almost the last trace of their labour was gone!

Even the foundations were partially destroyed. And in rebuilding it they could not this time, as before, make use of the fallen stones. This time the stones had vanished too. The force of the explosion had flung them to distances of hundreds of yards. It was as though the windmill had never been.

As they approached the farm Squealer, who had unaccountably been absent during the fighting, came skipping towards them, whisking his tail and beaming with satisfaction. And the animals heard, from the direction of the farm buildings, the solemn booming of a gun.

"What is that gun firing for?" said Boxer. "To

celebrate our victory!" cried Squealer.

"What victory?" said Boxer. His knees were bleeding, he had lost a shoe and split his hoof, and a dozen pellets had lodged themselves in his hind leg.

"What victory, comrade? Have we not driven the enemy off our soil — the sacred soil of Animal Farm?"

"But they have destroyed the windmill. And we had worked on it for two years!"

"What matter? We will build another windmill. We will build six windmills if we feel like it. You do not appreciate, comrade, the mighty thing that we have done. The enemy was in occupation of this very ground that we stand upon. And now — thanks to the leadership of Comrade Napoleon — we have won every inch of it back again!"

"Then we have won back what we had before," said Boxer. "That is our victory," said Squealer.

They limped into the yard. The pellets under the skin of Boxer's leg smarted painfully. He saw ahead of him the heavy labour of rebuilding the windmill from the foundations, and already in imagination he braced himself for the task. But for the first time it occurred to him that he was eleven years old and that perhaps his great muscles were not quite what they had once been.

But when the animals saw the green flag flying, and heard the gun firing again — seven times it was fired in all

— and heard the speech that Napoleon made, congratulating them on their conduct, it did seem to them after all that they had won a great victory. The animals slain in the battle were given a solemn funeral. Boxer and Clover pulled the wagon which served as a hearse, and Napoleon himself walked at the head of the procession. Two whole days were given over to celebrations. There were songs, speeches, and more firing of the gun, and a special gift of an apple was bestowed on every animal, with two ounces of corn for each bird and three biscuits for each dog. It was announced that the battle would be called the Battle of the Windmill, and that Napoleon had created a new decoration, the Order of the Green Banner, which he had conferred upon himself. In the general rejoicings the unfortunate affair of the banknotes was forgotten.

It was a few days later than this that the pigs came upon a case of whisky in the cellars of the farmhouse. It had been overlooked at the time when the house was first occupied. That night there came from the farmhouse the sound of loud singing, in which, to everyone's surprise, the strains of 'Beasts of England' were mixed up. At about half past nine Napoleon, wearing an old bowler hat of Mr. Jones's, was distinctly seen to emerge from the back door, gallop rapidly round the yard, and disappear indoors again. But in the morning a deep silence hung over the farmhouse. Not a pig appeared to be stirring. It was nearly

nine o'clock when Squealer made his appearance, walking slowly and dejectedly, his eyes dull, his tail hanging limply behind him, and with every appearance of being seriously ill. He called the animals together and told them that he had a terrible piece of news to impart. Comrade Napoleon was dying!

A cry of lamentation went up. Straw was laid down outside the doors of the farmhouse, and the animals walked on tiptoe. With tears in their eyes they asked one another what they should do if their Leader were taken away from them. A rumour went round that Snowball had after all contrived to introduce poison into Napoleon's food. At eleven o'clock Squealer came out to make another announcement. As his last act upon earth, Comrade Napoleon had pronounced a solemn decree: the drinking of alcohol was to be punished by death.

By the evening, however, Napoleon appeared to be somewhat better, and the following morning Squealer was able to tell them that he was well on the way to recovery. By the evening of that day Napoleon was back at work, and on the next day it was learned that he had instructed Whymper to purchase in Willingdon some booklets on brewing and distilling. A week later Napoleon gave orders that the small paddock beyond the orchard, which it had previously been intended to set aside as a grazing-ground for animals who were past work, was to be ploughed up. It was given out that the pasture was exhausted and needed re-seeding; but it soon became known that Napoleon intended to sow it with barley.

About this time there occurred a strange incident which hardly anyone was able to understand. One night at about twelve o'clock there was a loud crash in the yard, and the animals rushed out of their stalls. It was a moonlit night. At the foot of the end wall of the big barn, where the Seven Commandments were written, there lay a ladder broken in two pieces. Squealer, temporarily stunned, was sprawling beside it, and near at hand there lay a lantern, a paint-brush, and an overturned pot of white paint. The dogs immediately made a ring round Squealer, and escorted him back to the farmhouse as soon as he was able to walk. None of the animals could form any idea as to what this meant, except old Benjamin, who nodded his muzzle with a knowing air, and seemed to understand, but would say nothing.

But a few days later Muriel, reading over the Seven Commandments to herself, noticed that there was yet another of them which the animals had remembered wrong. They had thought the Fifth Commandment was "No animal shall drink alcohol," but there were two words that they had forgotten. Actually the Commandment read: "No animal shall drink alcohol TO EXCESS."

CHAPTER 9

Boxer's split hoof was a long time in healing. They had started the rebuilding of the windmill the day after the victory celebrations were ended. Boxer refused to take even a day off work, and made it a point of honour not to let it be seen that he was in pain. In the evenings he would admit privately to Clover that the hoof troubled him a great deal. Clover treated the hoof with poultices of herbs which she prepared by chewing them, and both she and Benjamin urged Boxer to work less hard. "A horse's lungs do not last for ever," she said to him. But Boxer would not listen. He had, he said, only one real ambition left — to see the windmill well under way before he reached the age for retirement.

At the beginning, when the laws of Animal Farm were first formulated, the retiring age had been fixed for horses and pigs at twelve, for cows at fourteen, for dogs at nine, for sheep at seven, and for hens and geese at five. Liberal old-age pensions had been agreed upon. As yet no animal had actually retired on pension, but of late the subject had

been discussed more and more. Now that the small field beyond the orchard had been set aside for barley, it was rumoured that a corner of the large pasture was to be fenced off and turned into a grazing-ground for superannuated animals. For a horse, it was said, the pension would be five pounds of corn a day and, in winter, fifteen pounds of hay, with a carrot or possibly an apple on public holidays. Boxer's twelfth birthday was due in the late summer of the following year.

Meanwhile life was hard. The winter was as cold as the last one had been, and food was even shorter. Once again all rations were reduced, except those of the pigs and the dogs. A too rigid equality in rations, Squealer explained, would have been contrary to the principles of Animalism. In any case he had no difficulty in proving to the other animals that they were NOT in reality short of food, whatever the appearances might be. For the time being, certainly, it had been found necessary to make a readjustment of rations (Squealer always spoke of it as a "readjustment," never as a "reduction"), but in comparison with the days of Jones, the improvement was enormous. Reading out the figures in a shrill, rapid voice, he proved to them in detail that they had more oats, more hay, more turnips than they had had in Jones's day, that they worked shorter hours, that their drinking water was of better quality, that they lived longer, that a larger proportion

of their young ones survived infancy, and that they had more straw in their stalls and suffered less from fleas. The animals believed every word of it. Truth to tell, Jones and all he stood for had almost faded out of their memories. They knew that life nowadays was harsh and bare, that they were often hungry and often cold, and that they were usually working when they were not asleep. But doubtless it had been worse in the old days. They were glad to believe so. Besides, in those days they had been slaves and now they were free, and that made all the difference, as Squealer did not fail to point out.

There were many more mouths to feed now. In the autumn the four sows had all littered about simultaneously, producing thirty-one young pigs between them. The young pigs were piebald, and as Napoleon was the only boar on the farm, it was possible to guess at their parentage. It was announced that later, when bricks and timber had been purchased, a schoolroom would be built in the farmhouse garden. For the time being, the young pigs were given their instruction by Napoleon himself in the farmhouse kitchen. They took their exercise in the garden, and were discouraged from playing with the other young animals. About this time, too, it was laid down as a rule that when a pig and any other animal met on the path, the other animal must stand aside: and also that all pigs, of whatever degree, were to have the privilege of wearing green ribbons on

their tails on Sundays.

The farm had had a fairly successful year, but was still short of money. There were the bricks, sand, and lime for the schoolroom to be purchased, and it would also be necessary to begin saving up again for the machinery for the windmill. Then there were lamp oil and candles for the house, sugar for Napoleon's own table (he forbade this to the other pigs, on the ground that it made them fat), and all the usual replacements such as tools, nails, string, coal, wire, scrap-iron, and dog biscuits. A stump of hay and part of the potato crop were sold off, and the contract for eggs was increased to six hundred a week, so that that year the hens barely hatched enough chicks to keep their numbers at the same level. Rations, reduced in December, were reduced again in February, and lanterns in the stalls were forbidden to save oil. But the pigs seemed comfortable enough, and in fact were putting on weight if anything. One afternoon in late February a warm, rich, appetising scent, such as the animals had never smelt before, wafted itself across the yard from the little brew-house, which had been disused in Jones's time, and which stood beyond the kitchen. Someone said it was the smell of cooking barley. The animals sniffed the air hungrily and wondered whether a warm mash was being prepared for their supper. But no warm mash appeared, and on the following Sunday it was announced that from now onwards all barley would be

reserved for the pigs. The field beyond the orchard had already been sown with barley. And the news soon leaked out that every pig was now receiving a ration of a pint of beer daily, with half a gallon for Napoleon himself, which was always served to him in the Crown Derby soup tureen.

But if there were hardships to be borne, they were partly offset by the fact that life nowadays had a greater dignity than it had had before.

There were more songs, more speeches, more processions. Napoleon had commanded that once a week there should be held something called a Spontaneous Demonstration, the object of which was to celebrate the struggles and triumphs of Animal Farm. At the appointed time the animals would leave their work and march round the precincts of the farm in military formation, with the pigs leading, then the horses, then the cows, then the sheep, and then the poultry. The dogs flanked the procession and at the head of all marched Napoleon's black cockerel.

Boxer and Clover always carried between them a green banner marked with the hoof and the horn and the caption, "Long live Comrade Napoleon!" Afterwards there were recitations of poems composed in Napoleon's honour, and a speech by Squealer giving particulars of the latest increases in the production of foodstuffs, and on occasion a shot was fired from the gun. The sheep were the greatest devotees of the Spontaneous Demonstration, and if anyone complained (as a few animals sometimes did, when no pigs or dogs were near) that they wasted time and meant a lot of standing about in the cold, the sheep were sure to silence him with a tremendous bleating of "Four legs good, two legs bad!" But by and large the animals enjoyed these celebrations. They found it comforting to be reminded that, after all, they were truly their own masters and that the work they did was for their own benefit. So that, what with the songs, the processions, Squealer's lists of figures, the thunder of the gun, the crowing of the cockerel, and the fluttering of the flag, they were able to forget that their bellies were empty, at least part of the time.

In April, Animal Farm was proclaimed a Republic, and it became necessary to elect a President. There was only one candidate, Napoleon, who was elected unanimously. On the same day it was given out that fresh documents had been discovered which revealed further details about Snowball's complicity with Jones. It now appeared that Snowball had not, as the animals had previously imagined, merely attempted to lose the Battle of the Cowshed by means of a stratagem, but had been openly fighting on Jones's side. In fact, it was he who had actually been the leader of the human forces, and had charged into battle with the words "Long live Humanity!" on his lips. The wounds on Snowball's back, which a few of the animals

still remembered to have seen, had been inflicted by Napoleon's teeth.

In the middle of the summer Moses the raven suddenly reappeared on the farm, after an absence of several years. He was quite unchanged, still did no work, and talked in the same strain as ever about Sugarcandy Mountain. He would perch on a stump, flap his black wings, and talk by the hour to anyone who would listen. "Up there, comrades," he would say solemnly, pointing to the sky with his large beak — "up there, just on the other side of that dark cloud that you can see — there it lies, Sugarcandy Mountain, that happy country where we poor animals shall rest for ever from our labours!" He even claimed to have been there on one of his higher flights, and to have seen the everlasting fields of clover and the linseed cake and lump sugar growing on the hedges. Many of the animals believed him. Their lives now, they reasoned, were hungry and laborious; was it not right and just that a better world should exist somewhere else? A thing that was difficult to determine was the attitude of the pigs towards Moses. They all declared contemptuously that his stories about Sugarcandy Mountain were lies, and yet they allowed him to remain on the farm, not working, with an allowance of a gill of beer a day.

After his hoof had healed up, Boxer worked harder than ever. Indeed, all the animals worked like slaves that

year. Apart from the regular work of the farm, and the rebuilding of the windmill, there was the schoolhouse for the young pigs, which was started in March. Sometimes the long hours on insufficient food were hard to bear, but Boxer never faltered. In nothing that he said or did was there any sign that his strength was not what it had been. It was only his appearance that was a little altered; his hide was less shiny than it had used to be, and his great haunches seemed to have shrunken. The others said, "Boxer will pick up when the spring grass comes on"; but the spring came and Boxer grew no fatter.

Sometimes on the slope leading to the top of the quarry, when he braced his muscles against the weight of some vast boulder, it seemed that nothing kept him on his feet except the will to continue. At such times his lips were seen to form the words, "I will work harder"; he had no voice left. Once again Clover and Benjamin warned him to take care of his health, but Boxer paid no attention. His twelfth birthday was approaching. He did not care what happened so long as a good store of stone was accumulated before he went on pension.

Late one evening in the summer, a sudden rumour ran round the farm that something had happened to Boxer. He had gone out alone to drag a load of stone down to the windmill. And sure enough, the rumour was true. A few minutes later two pigeons came racing in with the news;

"Boxer has fallen! He is lying on his side and can't get up!"

About half the animals on the farm rushed out to the knoll where the windmill stood. There lay Boxer, between the shafts of the cart, his neck stretched out, unable even to raise his head. His eyes were glazed, his sides matted with sweat. A thin stream of blood had trickled out of his mouth. Clover dropped to her knees at his side.

"Boxer!" she cried, "how are you?"

"It is my lung," said Boxer in a weak voice. "It does not matter. I think you will be able to finish the windmill without me. There is a pretty good store of stone accumulated. I had only another month to go in any case. To tell you the truth, I had been looking forward to my retirement. And perhaps, as Benjamin is growing old too, they will let him retire at the same time and be a companion to me."

"We must get help at once," said Clover. "Run, somebody, and tell Squealer what has happened."

All the other animals immediately raced back to the farmhouse to give Squealer the news. Only Clover remained, and Benjamin who lay down at Boxer's side, and, without speaking, kept the flies off him with his long tail. After about a quarter of an hour Squealer appeared, full of sympathy and concern. He said that Comrade Napoleon had learned with the very deepest distress of this

misfortune to one of the most loyal workers on the farm, and was already making arrangements to send Boxer to be treated in the hospital at Willingdon. The animals felt a little uneasy at this. Except for Mollie and Snowball, no other animal had ever left the farm, and they did not like to think of their sick comrade in the hands of human beings. However, Squealer easily convinced them that the veterinary surgeon in Willingdon could treat Boxer's case more satisfactorily than could be done on the farm. And about half an hour later, when Boxer had somewhat recovered, he was with difficulty got on to his feet, and managed to limp back to his stall, where Clover and Benjamin had prepared a good bed of straw for him.

For the next two days Boxer remained in his stall. The pigs had sent out a large bottle of pink medicine which they had found in the medicine chest in the bathroom, and Clover administered it to Boxer twice a day after meals. In the evenings she lay in his stall and talked to him, while Benjamin kept the flies off him. Boxer professed not to be sorry for what had happened. If he made a good recovery, he might expect to live another three years, and he looked forward to the peaceful days that he would spend in the corner of the big pasture. It would be the first time that he had had leisure to study and improve his mind. He intended, he said, to devote the rest of his life to learning the remaining twenty-two letters of the alphabet.

However, Benjamin and Clover could only be with Boxer after working hours, and it was in the middle of the day when the van came to take him away. The animals were all at work weeding turnips under the supervision of a pig, when they were astonished to see Benjamin come galloping from the direction of the farm buildings, braying at the top of his voice. It was the first time that they had ever seen Benjamin excited — indeed, it was the first time that anyone had ever seen him gallop. "Quick, quick!" he shouted. "Come at once! They're taking Boxer away!" Without waiting for orders from the pig, the animals broke off work and raced back to the farm buildings. Sure enough, there in the yard was a large closed van, drawn by two horses, with lettering on its side and a sly-looking man in a low-crowned bowler hat sitting on the driver's seat. And Boxer's stall was empty.

The animals crowded round the van. "Good-bye, Boxer!" they chorused, "good-bye!"

"Fools! Fools!" shouted Benjamin, prancing round them and stamping the earth with his small hoofs. "Fools! Do you not see what is written on the side of that van?"

That gave the animals pause, and there was a hush. Muriel began to spell out the words. But Benjamin pushed her aside and in the midst of a deadly silence he read:

" 'Alfred Simmonds, Horse Slaughterer and Glue Boiler, Willingdon. Dealer in Hides and Bone-Meal.

242

Kennels Supplied.' Do you not understand what that means? They are taking Boxer to the knacker's!"

A cry of horror burst from all the animals. At this moment the man on the box whipped up his horses and the van moved out of the yard at a smart trot. All the animals followed, crying out at the tops of their voices. Clover forced her way to the front. The van began to gather speed. Clover tried to stir her stout limbs to a gallop, and achieved a canter. "Boxer!" she cried. "Boxer! Boxer! Boxer!" And just at this moment, as though he had heard the uproar outside, Boxer's face, with the white stripe down his nose, appeared at the small window at the back of the van.

"Boxer!" cried Clover in a terrible voice. "Boxer! Get out! Get out quickly! They're taking you to your death!"

All the animals took up the cry of "Get out, Boxer, get out!" But the van was already gathering speed and drawing away from them. It was uncertain whether Boxer had understood what Clover had said. But a moment later his face disappeared from the window and there was the sound of a tremendous drumming of hoofs inside the van. He was trying to kick his way out. The time had been when a few kicks from Boxer's hoofs would have smashed the van to matchwood. But alas! his strength had left him; and in a few moments the sound of drumming hoofs grew

fainter and died away. In desperation the animals began
appealing to the two horses which drew the van to stop.
"Comrades, comrades!" they shouted. "Don't take your
own brother to his death! "But the stupid brutes, too
ignorant to realise what was happening, merely set back
their ears and quickened their pace. Boxer's face did
not reappear at the window. Too late,

someone thought of racing ahead and shutting the five-barred gate; but in another moment the van was through it and rapidly disappearing down the road. Boxer was never seen again.

Three days later it was announced that he had died in the hospital at Willingdon, in spite of receiving every attention a horse could have. Squealer came to announce the news to the others. He had, he said, been present during Boxer's last hours.

"It was the most affecting sight I have ever seen!" said Squealer, lifting his trotter and wiping away a tear. "I was at his bedside at the very last. And at the end, almost too weak to speak, he whispered in my ear that his sole sorrow was to have passed on before the windmill was finished. 'Forward, comrades!' he whispered. 'Forward in the name of the Rebellion. Long live Animal Farm! Long live Comrade Napoleon! Napoleon is always right.' Those were his very last words, comrades."

Here Squealer's demeanour suddenly changed. He fell silent for a moment, and his little eyes darted suspicious glances from side to side before he proceeded.

It had come to his knowledge, he said, that a foolish and wicked rumour had been circulated at the time of Boxer's removal. Some of the animals had noticed that the van which took Boxer away was marked "Horse

Slaughterer," and had actually jumped to the conclusion that Boxer was being sent to the knacker's. It was almost unbelievable, said Squealer, that any animal could be so stupid. Surely, he cried indignantly, whisking his tail and skipping from side to side, surely they knew their beloved Leader, Comrade Napoleon, better than that? But the explanation was really very simple. The van had previously been the property of the knacker, and had been bought by the veterinary surgeon, who had not yet painted the old name out. That was how the mistake had arisen.

The animals were enormously relieved to hear this. And when Squealer went on to give further graphic details of Boxer's death-bed, the admirable care he had received, and the expensive medicines for which Napoleon had paid without a thought as to the cost, their last doubts disappeared and the sorrow that they felt for their comrade's death was tempered by the thought that at least he had died happy.

Napoleon himself appeared at the meeting on the following Sunday morning and pronounced a short oration in Boxer's honour. It had not been possible, he said, to bring back their lamented comrade's remains for interment on the farm, but he had ordered a large wreath to be made from the laurels in the farmhouse garden and sent down to be placed on Boxer's grave. And in a few days' time the pigs intended to hold a memorial banquet in Boxer's honour.

Napoleon ended his speech with a reminder of Boxer's two favourite maxims, "I will work harder" and "Comrade Napoleon is always right" — maxims, he said, which every animal would do well to adopt as his own.

On the day appointed for the banquet, a grocer's van drove up from Willingdon and delivered a large wooden crate at the farmhouse. That night there was the sound of uproarious singing, which was followed by what sounded like a violent quarrel and ended at about eleven o'clock with a tremendous crash of glass. No one stirred in the farmhouse before noon on the following day, and the word went round that from somewhere or other the pigs had acquired the money to buy themselves another case of whisky.

CHAPTER 10

Years passed. The seasons came and went, the short animal lives fled by. A time came when there was no one who remembered the old days before the Rebellion, except Clover, Benjamin, Moses the raven, and a number of the pigs.

Muriel was dead; Bluebell, Jessie, and Pincher were dead. Jones too was dead — he had died in an inebriates' home in another part of the country. Snowball was forgotten. Boxer was forgotten, except by the few who had known him. Clover was an old stout mare now, stiff in the joints and with a tendency to rheumy eyes. She was two years past the retiring age, but in fact no animal had ever actually retired. The talk of setting aside a corner of the pasture for superannuated animals had long since been dropped. Napoleon was now a mature boar of twenty-four stone.

Squealer was so fat that he could with difficulty see out of his eyes. Only old Benjamin was much the same as ever, except for being a little greyer about the muzzle, and, since

Boxer's death, more morose and taciturn than ever.

There were many more creatures on the farm now, though the increase was not so great as had been expected in earlier years. Many animals had been born to whom the Rebellion was only a dim tradition, passed on by word of mouth, and others had been bought who had never heard mention of such a thing before their arrival. The farm possessed three horses now besides Clover. They were fine upstanding beasts, willing workers and good comrades, but very stupid. None of them proved able to learn the alphabet beyond the letter B. They accepted everything that they were told about the Rebellion and the principles of Animalism, especially from Clover, for whom they had an almost filial respect; but it was doubtful whether they understood very much of it.

The farm was more prosperous now, and better organised: it had even been enlarged by two fields which had been bought from Mr. Pilkington. The windmill had been successfully completed at last, and the farm possessed a threshing machine and a hay elevator of its own, and various new buildings had been added to it. Whymper had bought himself a dogcart. The windmill, however, had not after all been used for generating electrical power. It was used for milling corn, and brought in a handsome money profit. The animals were hard at work building yet another windmill; when that one was finished, so it was said, the

dynamos would be installed. But the luxuries of which Snowball had once taught the animals to dream, the stalls with electric light and hot and cold water, and the three-day week, were no longer talked about.

Napoleon had denounced such ideas as contrary to the spirit of Animalism. The truest happiness, he said, lay in working hard and living frugally.

Somehow it seemed as though the farm had grown richer without making the animals themselves any richer- except, of course, for the pigs and the dogs. Perhaps this was partly because there were so many pigs and so many dogs. It was not that these creatures did not work, after their fashion. There was, as Squealer was never tired of explaining, endless work in the supervision and organisation of the farm. Much of this work was of a kind that the other animals were too ignorant to understand. For example, Squealer told them that the pigs had to expend enormous labours every day upon mysterious things called "files," "reports," "minutes," and "memoranda". These were large sheets of paper which had to be closely covered with writing, and as soon as they were so covered, they were burnt in the furnace. This was of the highest importance for the welfare of the farm, Squealer said. But still, neither pigs nor dogs produced any food by their own labour; and there were very many of them, and their appetites were always good.

As for the others, their life, so far as they knew, was as it had always been. They were generally hungry, they slept on straw, they drank from the pool, they laboured in the fields; in winter they were troubled by the cold, and in summer by the flies. Sometimes the older ones among them racked their dim memories and tried to determine whether in the early days of the Rebellion, when Jones's expulsion was still recent, things had been better or worse than now. They could not remember. There was nothing with which they could compare their present lives: they had nothing to go upon except Squealer's lists of figures, which invariably demonstrated that everything was getting better and better. The animals found the problem insoluble; in any case, they had little time for speculating on such things now. Only old Benjamin professed to remember every detail of his long life and to know that things never had been, nor ever could be much better or much worse — hunger, hardship, and disappointment being, so he said, the unalterable law of life.

And yet the animals never gave up hope. More, they never lost, even for an instant, their sense of honour and privilege in being members of Animal Farm. They were still the only farm in the whole county — in all England! — owned and operated by animals. Not one of them, not even the youngest, not even the newcomers who had been brought from farms ten or twenty miles away, ever ceased

to marvel at that. And when they heard the gun booming and saw the green flag fluttering at the masthead, their hearts swelled with imperishable pride, and the talk turned always towards the old heroic days, the expulsion of Jones, the writing of the Seven Commandments, the great battles in which the human invaders had been defeated. None of the old dreams had been abandoned. The Republic of the Animals which Major had foretold, when the green fields of England should be untrodden by human feet, was still believed in. Some day it was coming: it might not be soon, it might not be with in the lifetime of any animal now living, but still it was coming. Even the tune of 'Beasts of England' was perhaps hummed secretly here and there: at any rate, it was a fact that every animal on the farm knew it, though no one would have dared to sing it aloud. It might be that their lives were hard and that not all of their hopes had been fulfilled; but they were conscious that they were not as other animals. If they went hungry, it was not from feeding tyrannical human beings; if they worked hard, at least they worked for themselves. No creature among them went upon two legs. No creature called any other creature "Master." All animals were equal.

One day in early summer Squealer ordered the sheep to follow him, and led them out to a piece of waste ground at the other end of the farm, which had become overgrown with birch saplings. The sheep spent the whole day there browsing at the leaves under Squealer's supervision. In the evening he returned to the farmhouse himself, but, as it was warm weather, told the sheep to stay where they were. It ended by their remaining there for a whole week, during which time the other animals saw nothing of them. Squealer was with them for the greater part of every day. He was, he said, teaching them to sing a new song, for which privacy was needed.

It was just after the sheep had returned, on a pleasant evening when the animals had finished work and were making their way back to the farm buildings, that the terrified neighing of a horse sounded from the yard. Startled, the animals stopped in their tracks. It was Clover's voice. She neighed again, and all the animals broke into a gallop and rushed into the yard. Then they saw what Clover had seen.

It was a pig walking on his hind legs.

Yes, it was Squealer. A little awkwardly, as though not quite used to supporting his considerable bulk in that position, but with perfect balance, he was strolling across the yard. And a moment later, out from the door of the farmhouse came a long file of pigs, all walking on their hind legs. Some did it better than others, one or two were even a trifle unsteady and looked as though they would have liked the support of a stick, but every one of them made his way right round the yard successfully. And finally there was a

tremendous baying of
dogs and a shrill crowing
from the black cockerel,
and out came Napoleon
himself, majestically upright,
casting haughty glances from
side to side, and with his
dogs gambolling round him.

He carried a whip in
his trotter.

There was a deadly
silence. Amazed, terrified,
huddling together, the animals watched the long line of
pigs march slowly round the yard. It was as though the
world had turned upside-down. Then there came a moment
when the first shock had worn off and when, in spite of
everything-in spite of their terror of the dogs, and of the
habit, developed through long years, of never complaining,
never criticising, no matter what happened — they might
have uttered some word of protest. But just at that
moment, as though at a signal, all the sheep burst out into
a tremendous bleating of — "Four legs good, two legs
BETTER! Four legs good, two legs BETTER! Four legs
good, two legs BETTER!"

It went on for five minutes without stopping. And by
the time the sheep had quieted down, the chance to utter

any protest had passed, for the pigs had marched back into the farmhouse.

Benjamin felt a nose nuzzling at his shoulder. He looked round. It was Clover. Her old eyes looked dimmer than ever. Without saying anything, she tugged gently at his mane and led him round to the end of the big barn, where the Seven Commandments were written. For a minute or two they stood gazing at the tatted wall with its white lettering.

"My sight is failing," she said finally. "Even when I was young I could not have read what was written there. But it appears to me that that wall looks different. Are the Seven Commandments the same as they used to be, Benjamin?"

For once Benjamin consented to break his rule, and he read out to her what was written on the wall. There was nothing there now except a single Commandment. It ran:

ALL ANIMALS ARE EQUAL
BUT SOME ANIMALS ARE MORE EQUAL
THAN OTHERS

After that it did not seem strange when next day the pigs who were supervising the work of the farm all carried whips in their trotters. It did not seem strange to learn that the pigs had bought themselves a wireless set, were arranging to install a telephone, and had taken out subscriptions to 'John Bull', 'Tit-Bits', and the 'Daily Mirror'. It did not seem strange when Napoleon was seen strolling in the farmhouse garden with a pipe in his mouth — no, not even when the pigs took Mr. Jones's clothes out of the wardrobes and put them on, Napoleon himself appearing in a black coat, ratcatcher breeches, and leather leggings, while his favourite sow appeared in the watered silk dress which Mrs. Jones had been used to wearing on Sundays.

A week later, in the afternoon, a number of dog-carts drove up to the farm. A deputation of neighbouring farmers had been invited to make a tour of inspection. They were shown all over the farm, and expressed great admiration for everything they saw, especially the windmill. The animals were weeding the turnip field. They worked diligently hardly raising their faces from the ground, and not knowing whether to be more frightened of the pigs or of the human visitors.

That evening loud laughter and bursts of singing came from the farmhouse. And suddenly, at the sound of the mingled voices, the animals were stricken with curiosity.

What could be happening in there, now that for the first time animals and human beings were meeting on terms of equality? With one accord they began to creep as quietly as possible into the farmhouse garden.

At the gate they paused, half frightened to go on but Clover led the way in. They tiptoed up to the house, and such animals as were tall enough peered in at the dining-room window. There, round the long table, sat half a dozen farmers and half a dozen of the more eminent pigs, Napoleon himself occupying the seat of honour at the head of the table. The pigs appeared completely at ease in their chairs. The company had been enjoying a game of cards but had broken off for the moment, evidently in order to drink

a toast. A large jug was circulating, and the mugs were being refilled with beer. No one noticed the wondering faces of the animals that gazed in at the window.

Mr. Pilkington, of Foxwood, had stood up, his mug in his hand. In a moment, he said, he would ask the present company to drink a toast. But before doing so, there were a few words that he felt it incumbent upon him to say.

It was a source of great satisfaction to him, he said — and, he was sure, to all others present — to feel that a long period of mistrust and misunderstanding had now come to an end. There had been a time — not that he, or any of the present company, had shared such sentiments — but there had been a time when the respected proprietors of Animal Farm had been regarded, he would not say with hostility, but perhaps with a certain measure of misgiving, by their human neighbours.

Unfortunate incidents had occurred, mistaken ideas had been current. It had been felt that the existence of a farm owned and operated by pigs was somehow abnormal and was liable to have an unsettling effect in the neighbourhood. Too many farmers had assumed, without due enquiry, that on such a farm a spirit of licence and indiscipline would prevail.

They had been nervous about the effects upon their own animals, or even upon their human employees. But all such doubts were now dispelled.

Today he and his friends had visited Animal Farm and inspected every inch of it with their own eyes, and what did they find? Not only the most up-to-date methods, but a discipline and an orderliness which should be an example to all farmers everywhere. He believed that he was right in saying that the lower animals on Animal Farm did more work and received less food than any animals in the county. Indeed, he and his fellow-visitors today had observed many features which they intended to introduce on their own farms immediately.

He would end his remarks, he said, by emphasising once again the friendly feelings that subsisted, and ought to subsist, between Animal Farm and its neighbours. Between pigs and human beings there was not, and there need not be, any clash of interests whatever. Their struggles and their difficulties were one. Was not the labour problem the same everywhere? Here it became apparent that Mr. Pilkington was about to spring some carefully prepared witticism on the company, but for a moment he was too overcome by amusement to be able to utter it. After much choking, during which his various chins turned purple, he managed to get it out: "If you have your lower animals to contend with," he said, "we have our lower classes!" This BON MOT set the table in a roar; and Mr. Pilkington once again congratulated the pigs on the low rations, the long working hours, and the general absence of pampering

which he had observed on Animal Farm.

And now, he said finally, he would ask the company to rise to their feet and make certain that their glasses were full. "Gentlemen," concluded Mr. Pilkington, "gentlemen, I give you a toast: To the prosperity of Animal Farm!"

There was enthusiastic cheering and stamping of feet. Napoleon was so gratified that he left his place and came round the table to clink his mug against Mr. Pilkington's before emptying it. When the cheering had died down, Napoleon, who had remained on his feet, intimated that he too had a few words to say.

Like all of Napoleon's speeches, it was short and to the point. He too, he said, was happy that the period of misunderstanding was at an end. For a long time there had been rumours — circulated, he had reason to think, by some malignant enemy — that there was something subversive and even revolutionary in the outlook of himself and his colleagues. They had been credited with attempting to stir up rebellion among the animals on neighbouring farms. Nothing could be further from the truth! Their sole wish, now and in the past, was to live at peace and in normal business relations with their neighbours. This farm which he had the honour to control, he added, was a co-operative enterprise. The title-deeds, which were in his own possession, were owned by the pigs jointly.

He did not believe, he said, that any of the old suspicions still lingered, but certain changes had been made recently in the routine of the farm which should have the effect of promoting confidence still further.

Hitherto the animals on the farm had had a rather foolish custom of addressing one another as "Comrade." This was to be suppressed. There had also been a very strange custom, whose origin was unknown, of marching every Sunday morning past a boar's skull which was nailed to a post in the garden. This, too, would be suppressed, and the skull had already been buried. His visitors might have observed, too, the green flag which flew from the masthead. If so, they would perhaps have noted that the white hoof and horn with which it had previously been marked had now been removed. It would be a plain green flag from now onwards.

He had only one criticism, he said, to make of Mr. Pilkington's excellent and neighbourly speech. Mr. Pilkington had referred throughout to "Animal Farm." He could not of course know — for he, Napoleon, was only now for the first time announcing it — that the name "Animal Farm" had been abolished. Henceforward the farm was to be known as "The Manor Farm" — which, he believed, was its correct and original name.

"Gentlemen," concluded Napoleon, "I will give you the same toast as before, but in a different form. Fill

your glasses to the brim. Gentlemen, here is my toast: To
the prosperity of The Manor Farm!"

There was the same hearty cheering as before, and the
mugs were emptied to the dregs. But as the animals outside
gazed at the scene, it seemed to them that some strange
thing was happening. What was it that had altered in the
faces of the pigs? Clover's old dim eyes flitted from one
face to another. Some of them had five chins, some had
four, some had three. But what was it that seemed to be
melting and changing? Then, the applause having come to
an end, the company took up their cards and continued the
game that had been interrupted, and the animals crept
silently away.

But they had not gone twenty yards when they stopped
short. An uproar of voices was coming from the
farmhouse. They rushed back and looked through the
window again. Yes, a violent quarrel was in progress. There
were shoutings, bangings on the table, sharp suspicious
glances, furious denials. The source of the trouble appeared
to be that Napoleon and Mr. Pilkington had each played an
ace of spades simultaneously.

Twelve voices were shouting in anger, and they were all
alike. No question, now, what had happened to the faces of
the pigs. The creatures outside looked from pig to man,
and from man to pig, and from pig to man again; but
already it was impossible to say which was which.

國家圖書館出版品預行編目資料

動物農莊 / 喬治‧歐威爾（George Orwell）作；
李立瑋譯.-- 三版 -- 臺中市：晨星，2019.11
　　面；　公分. -- （愛藏本；99）
中英雙語典藏版
譯自：Animal Farm
ISBN 978-986-443-936-2（精裝）

873.57　　　　　　　　　　　　108016856

愛藏本：99

動物農莊（中英雙語典藏版）
Animal Farm

作　　者｜喬治・歐威爾（George Orwell）
繪　　者｜楊宛靜
譯　　者｜李立瑋

責任編輯｜呂曉婕
封面設計｜鍾文君
美術設計｜黃偵瑜
文字校潤｜呂曉婕、謝宜真、陳智杰

創 辦 人｜陳銘民
發 行 所｜晨星出版有限公司
　　　　　407 台中市西屯區工業 30 路 1 號
　　　　　TEL:(04)23595820　FAX:(04)23550581
　　　　　https://star.morningstar.com.tw
　　　　　行政院新聞局局版台業字第 2500 號
法律顧問｜陳思成律師
初版日期｜2019 年 11 月 15 日
再版日期｜2023 年 03 月 15 日（三刷）
　ISBN｜978-986-443-936-2
　定價｜新台幣 260 元

讀者專線｜TEL：02-23672044 / 04-23595819#212
傳真專線｜FAX：02-23635741 / 04-23595493
讀者信箱｜E-mail：service@morningstar.com.tw
網路書店｜https://www.morningstar.com.tw
郵政劃撥｜15060393（知己圖書股份有限公司）

印　　刷｜上好印刷股份有限公司

填寫線上回函，立刻享有
晨星網路書店50元購書金

Printed in Taiwan, all rights reserved.
版權所有 ・ 翻印必究
（缺頁或破損的書，請寄回更換）